HALFBREED

HALFBREED

A WESTERN DOUBLE

UZZIAH MOUNTAIN MAN
BOOK FIVE

J.J. BONHAM

WOLFPACK
PUBLISHING
— EST 2013 —

HALFBREED

HALFBREED

1

It was going to take Uzziah and Immanuel about two weeks to get back to their mountain home, if they didn't hurry, and really, there was no reason to. If they were going back up to the cabins, which they planned on doing, then they barely had the shank of summer and the fall to get ready for winter.

They would travel the length of the Nebraska territories. The Pawnee, Omaha, Oto-Missouri, Lakota, and Cheyenne, the princes of the plains all lived in those territories, and avoiding them would be the best outcome, but probably that outcome was unlikely.

"What's our best chance of not comin' into contact with any Injuns?" Uzziah asked.

"That would be zero, as in we will come into contact, and none of them will be Crow, so we can forget about them being all nice and all," Immanuel said, "but it's the Pawnee what's got me worried."

"Why's that?" Uzziah asked.

"They ain't notional at all, they just want us dead."

Uzziah sat Shadow and thought about that. Injuns

who just wanted them dead, well, that wasn't anything to look forward to, now was it?

The first night out of the flatlands around the Missouri, after they'd left the girls, Gretchen and Grace with their folks, the Hannas, Uzziah had a dream. It was coming back to him now as they rode along. Sometimes, dreams were indelible in your memory, just crying out to be brought up, but this dream had been a little different. Uzziah had started back reading the Bible from cover to cover, and he was in the 42nd chapter of the book of Genesis. That's the chapter in which Joseph's brothers come to buy grain in Egypt and don't recognize their youngest brother, whom they sold into slavery, but Joseph recognized them.

Uzziah figured it was because of where he was in the Bible, in Genesis, that this dream had become entangled with the Bible. That wasn't a bad thing, it had happen before, but in the dream, which was about Immanuel, he had brothers who had done him wrong, and they were coming back to him because of something which had happened around their home. In the dream, Immanuel was the only one who could save them, but instead of helping, Immanuel had not forgiven his brothers like Joseph had, but simply gotten on his horse, Trevor, and ridden away.

What could the dream mean? Immanuel had never told Uzziah of any brothers, or any family for that matter. Whenever the subject of family came up, he'd brushed it off with some joke or other.

"Say, pard, tell me 'bout yer family again," Uzziah said, riding easily beside his partner.

Immanuel just turned his head and looked at Uzziah as if he were speaking Chinese.

"Yer family, tell me more 'bout 'em," Uzziah encouraged.

"I ain't never talk to you 'bout no family, young son, and ya'll probably never hear me talkin' 'bout no family, since I ain't got any," he said, and he looked ahead confidently as if that was the end of the subject.

"But I had this chere dream—"

"Uh huh."

"Yer family—"

"No family, young son, none, zero kin. Are ya listenin' to me?"

"Then why would I have this chere dream 'bout 'em?"

"How in tarnation should I know? Ifn I had a dream 'bout some gal who wanted me to bed her, would that mean there was such a girl?"

"In yer case, it would mean that."

"Okay, okay, okay, I got ya. So, bad example," he said, and it looked like he was searching for a more appropriated example. "Okay, okay, ifn I had a dream 'bout a strong box with cash in it, would that mean there was such a strong box?"

"Probably not."

"Well, there ya go, just a'cause ya had some damned dream 'bout me havin' family, it don't mean there are such folks, it simply don't."

"But the dream was so real," Uzziah said, trailing off.

"I'll betcha they was mean and awful people," Immanuel said, laughing.

"Why would ya say that?"

"I don't know, just did, were they mean and awful in the dream?"

"Yeah, they was, partner, they was awful," Uzziah said, thinking now that his dream had maybe been from the Holy Spirit and there was something to it all.

"Well, there ya go, good guess, huh?" Immanuel said and kicked up Trevor and rode ahead a bit.

———

They rode the rest of the day, staying off the ridges and keeping to the low country. They saw a band of Pawnee in the afternoon, watering their horses down by the creek, and fortunately, the Pawnee hadn't seen them. They waited back in a copse of trees till the band of Injuns moved on out, and as luck would have it, the Pawnee were going the opposite direction from the two mountain men.

When they made camp, it was a cold one. Immanuel thought it best to not make fire, which makes smoke, which Injuns see right off. They still had some of the grub that Arline, the girls' mother, had wrapped in a calico napkin, so they ate that. It was biscuits and ham.

"These ain't as good as yourn," Immanuel said.

"Really?"

"Yer just like some gal, yeah, really, but ya want me to say it again, don't ya. Ain't happy with a compliment, ya want it repeated, and maybe added to, don't ya?"

Uzziah looked at his partner, who was usually cantankerous, but not that cantankerous, but then again, maybe the subject earlier in the day had started stewing in him?

"No, it's just an expression, ya know, as in, *Really?*

That's all it is," Uzziah said, knowing the biscuits weren't as good as his.

"Sorry, don't know what came over me." It wasn't like Immanuel to apologize either. Uzziah felt sure he had gotten on Immanuel's last nerve concerning family, which he claimed didn't exist, and that's all there was to it.

"I gotcha with the family thing earlier in the day, didn't I?"

Immanuel cut his head so fast toward Uzziah that now, he knew that he was right, so he just pressed ahead, not knowing what would come of it.

"In my dream—"

"Oh my God, ya gonna start in on that damned dream, again!?!"

"There was a family who had this youngest son, and when danger came near them, he, the youngest boy, was called upon to deal with the danger. Started when he was a kid, and since his pa was no good and a drunk, if anything was gonna be done fer the family, it had to be the youngest boy."

"Boring!" Immanuel said and kept on eating.

"Finally, there came a situation in which the youngest boy traded his life to protect the brothers, the bad pa, and the ma. Not really like Joseph in the Bible, but tangled up with that there story, a bit."

"How so? I remember the story of Joseph, they sold their youngest brother, who was a braggart, and by the way, a dreamer like somebody I know, and when he made good years later, he got even with 'em," Immanuel said, which was not exactly what had happened in Genesis, but close.

"Anythin' like that ever happen to you and yer family?" Uzziah asked.

Immanuel got up and, walking right over to where Uzziah was sitting, he pulled out his Bowie and pointed it into Uzziah's face. "Yer crazy, or ya wanna be hurt, which is it?" Immanuel asked in a voice that was unmistakable for Immanuel's bad voice.

Uzziah went on eating and didn't say anything. Eventually, Immanuel went back and sat down, looking back at his partner. Uzziah wasn't sure what that look meant.

———

In the middle of the night, Immanuel had a dream. If he'd been awake, he would have been pissed that now, he was having a dream, but like most dreams, we're asleep and he wasn't afforded the luxury of his own anger at the dream. The dream frightened him, so when he awakened, he went over and sat closer to Uzziah, his Hawken across his lap.

He had dreamed of his family, and he was so angry at Uzziah for bringing things to the surface that had been long buried. He loved his partner, and they had great times together, if you put aside the time he'd been buried alive in the New Mexico territories, but the young man just being who he was had a habit of bringing stuff up that a man like Immanuel had thought were dead and buried a long time in the past. Immanuel shook his head, obviously and evidently, they weren't.

Before Uzziah got up, Immanuel scouted around on Trevor and decided that the Pawnee they had seen the day before were long gone, and if he was to ride with any purpose today, he would like to have coffee, grits, bacon, and biscuits. He thought it was safe to do so when he took off back toward their camp. As he got closer, the smoke from the breakfast fire was not really noticeable, but it was noticeable.

"What ya doin'?" he asked Uzziah, who had the Dutch oven in the coals and bacon sizzling on the fire.

"Figured ya was out scoutin' so I made breakfast," Uzziah said.

"But what ifn it weren't safe, what the? Ya just sent up enough smoke to get us kilt!" Immanuel barked.

"But there ain't no Injuns, right, no Pawnee, they've gone on, right?"

"Yeah, but ya didn't know that," Immanuel said.

"Kinda, I did. Saw ya sittin' there next to me last night, and when ya left kinda knew what ya was up to," Uzziah said, smiling.

Immanuel just shook his head and looked around as if perhaps he'd been wrong about the Pawnee.

"Relax and have some breakfast," Uzziah suggested.

———

They rode for two more days and were almost out of Pawnee territory. Immanuel hadn't forgotten his dream, nor the provocation which had been unleashed upon him in his sleep. He just wished Uzziah could mind his own business, and not stir shite up from the past, his past, his almost completely forgotten past.

This preoccupation with his past was keeping his mind off the present, and that was never a good idea, especially in Pawnee territory. Immanuel looked over at Uzziah, who seemed almost asleep in the saddle.

"Have ya been checking our backtrail?" he asked Uzziah.

Uzziah shook himself awake and looked at his partner, trying to remember exactly where they were and what they were up to. "Nah, I didn't sleep good last night," he said.

Immanuel's head was on a swivel, and he caught just a glimpse of riders on a ridge behind them, and then they were gone. Their distinctive headdress and hair gave them away immediately.

"Pawnee!" he yelled and kicked Trevor up into a trot, then a loop, then a gallop. Uzziah was right beside him since he was on the faster horse.

"Ya sure?" Uzziah yelled over to Immanuel.

"As death," Immanuel said, and Uzziah didn't like the sound of that.

Taking a good look at where they were, in the rolling hills of the Nebraska territory, with hills essentially all around them, Immanuel didn't feel good about their chances. Pawnee could be over the next ridge, they could cut south and they might be there, cut north and find them there, too. For sure, he knew the small band of braves he'd seen behind them on the ridge was to the east. Best to keep riding west, he thought, and looked back only to see that they had come from cover and the chase was on. If he had a horse as fast as Shadow, well, they would outrun the bunch, but Trevor, though reliable and a good horse for distances, was not what you'd call fast. He looked ahead and there was another band of them coming directly at them.

"Kill one, and we'll cut south," Immanuel said as he raised his Hawken and fired before Uzziah had even raised his. The brave he'd shot rolled off his pony and was trampled by the six other riders, make that five, as Uzziah fired and turned south behind his partner. Uzziah snuck a peek over his shoulder and saw a brave riding with only one arm, blood was spurting out and spraying the riders to his right. Finally, having lost enough blood, he slipped off his horse.

Now, both bands—Immanuel counted as quickly as he could, and they numbered around twenty—had joined together and were hightailing toward them with the screams which Injuns do, hoping to make the White man afraid. But Uzziah and Immanuel had heard lots of Injuns scream, and the Pawnee were no different than the rest. Their screams flew up behind them in the chase, as their horses drew closer.

It looked like there were a couple of rifles with the Pawnee, but mostly it was bow and arrow, lances, tomahawks, and warclubs. Didn't matter, once they caught you, all those would do the trick.

A rifle fired, and the bullet passed somewhere between Trevor and Shadow.

"They're tryin' fer the horses, let's take to yonder hills," Immanuel said, "and fix them good!"

The hills that Immanuel pointed to were bigger than the undulating hills they were on, and if they made it there, then they would have the high ground, always a good thing in battle.

Shadow did not like the Pawnee's screams, and he had put it up into race mode, and Uzziah realized he was outrunning his partner.

When he looked around, Immanuel was being ridden up on by the fastest of the Pawnee ponies, and an arrow was notched into the Pawnee's bow, but before he could shoot it, Immanuel ran Trevor right into the Pawnee's pony, causing the Pawnee riding it to reach down and grab the war bridal to keep from falling off. Trevor never missed a step, and as Uzziah slowed, Trevor and his partner caught up with them.

"Into the hills, behind those rocks, now!" Immanuel ordered, and the two mountain men flew to safety, well, at least for a moment. They were off their horses, Immanuel handing Trevor's reins to Uzziah as he took both horses back further in the rocks and secured them.

"Ya'll stay here, ya hear!" Uzziah advised both horses, who could have cared less as they began munching on some tall grasses that grew near the boulders. Before he got back to where Immanuel was, there was a shot fired from the Hawken, that damned Immanuel could load a weapon faster than anyone he'd ever seen, maybe instead of practicing his roping all the time, he should practice fast-loading, just a thought, Uzziah wondered.

"They's circlin' and tryin' to see ifn there's a way fer them to git behind us," Immanuel said, loading again, and firing again. He was a one-man army.

Uzziah took up a position not far from Immanuel and fired and hit a Pawnee's pony, unfortunately. The pony tumbled and crushed the warrior. *Well, that's one way*, Uzziah thought.

"Ya might try actually shooting the Pawnee, don't want 'em to think we ain't good shots." Immanuel raised his rifle and was about to shoot when he stopped. "They's ridin' off," he advised Uzziah, who, not being blind, could see that for himself. "But they ain't done. They saw yer horse and how fast he is, and they want that damn horse, that's fer sure."

The Pawnee rode back out of range, which was

quite far for the Hawken. They had recognized the long rifles of the White men and weren't taking any chances.

"They'll have a parley, then some damn fool youngin' will take a run at us, just to count coop," Immanuel said as he looked up into the sky. It was well into the afternoon, and the sunset was not that far away.

Uzziah noticed his partner looking at the position of the sun and commented on it, "Didn't ya tell me Injuns don't attack at night?"

"Yeah, I probably said that, but then again, what's the one thing I always say about Injuns, huh?"

"They're notional."

"Exactly, so maybe this group don't attack at night, then again, maybe this group is the only group of Pawnee who do. Yer guess is as good as mine."

"Can't we make a run fer it?"

Immanuel just looked at Uzziah. "Well, young son, with that hoss of yers ya could make a run fer it, and probably make it, but Trevor, ya saw what happened back there. He's a great hoss, don't get me wrong, but out-runnin' Injuns, not likely. But that don't mean ya can't go and leave me chere," Immanuel said and looked back at the Pawnee who were circling around, then one of the younger ones came riding like the wind straight at them!

"Well, here comes the one they'll tell stories about, at least fer now, do ya want 'em, or do I take him?"

"What if we didn't shoot him?" Uzziah asked.

"Well, he'd keep comin' till he had ridden back chere with us, and then we'd have a hand-to-hand fight on our menu."

"Maybe he'll realize we don't want any trouble?"

"Did ya just say what I think ya said?"

"Yes, I did."

"Then, I have wasted the last few years tryin' to teach ya anythin', I swear, thinkin' that Injuns will realize we don't want any trouble is like hopin' a boil will go away without poppin' it."

"Let's not shoot and see what happens," Uzziah said.

Immanuel just threw up his hands. "Okay, Jesus, let's do that."

The young brave, he couldn't have been more than 15-16 years old, rode up and was bracing himself for the shot, and when it didn't come, he rode closer, then several more from the band of twenty broke away and screaming started after him.

"Shall we wait and see if these next Injuns wanna have a tea party, or what?" Immanuel asked, his mouth a sarcastic slash in his face.

They started unloading on the one who was closest and then took two of the others who had thought maybe they'd get in on the action.

They weren't worried about their rear, at least not yet. The face of rocks which had decided to jump from the rolling hills a thousand years ago went straight up, and the width of those same rocks precluded Injuns riding up behind them, unless of course they wanted to take a couple of days to do so. It was a great position, higher than their enemy and almost impregnable, but there was no water, and that, for lack of anything else, meant the Pawnee probably knew all they really had to do was wait, unless, of course, they attacked at night.

"What was the moon like last night?" Immanuel asked Uzziah.

"You were the one up all night, don't ya remember?"

"It was out, but there were clouds, so all I saw was the light, how close to, or way from, full do ya reckon it is?"

"It was waning from full, but barely," Uzziah said. That was one thing his partner could always count on, he was a watcher of the skies, Uzziah was.

"That's good, we can shoot as long as it's up, then see what happens."

2

The moonrise followed a very lengthy sunset and was up nearly all night. The days were getting shorter, and summer was almost over. Immanuel kept thinking about the garden that he and Uzziah were planting, and wondered if that no-good Willet had finished what they had started, probably did, but only because Leah would have been on his ass to get it done. Still, didn't look like they were going to enjoy any of their efforts planting corn if they were left out on the plains with no scalps and deader than coyote poop. He tried not to think like that, but recently, he had begun to contemplate his mortality, which isn't a good sign in gunfighters, sheriffs, or mountainmen.

A man should just live as he lives, till he dies, but when the confrontation of Injuns was upon them, well, that, in Immanuel's opinion, wasn't a natural death. To be seized upon by folks who lived basically back in the Stone Age, and torn apart just so they could see how brave you were, not an appealing death. That got him started thinking about Standing Bear, and the fact that after this, he probably wouldn't be welcomed in her bed anyway, well, maybe, he was a good lay. Still, she had those kids, and he thought that part of her desperation in bed was the simple fact that she wanted more, not more of the hornpipe, but more kids! It seemed they always wanted more. He did not want to father a child, it simply wasn't in his path of life, so that was probably through, he and Standing Bear, yeah, all done, he reckoned.

Uzziah's Hawken went off, and Immanuel nearly peed himself.

"What is it?" Immanuel asked, checking to see if he did in fact piss himself.

"What was it, would be more likely. Saw something crawlin' over there, and I put a large hole in it," Uzziah said, smiling.

"That's my boy," Immanuel said, but thought, *what the hell, we got Injuns crawling toward us, and I'm worried about quim.* He should go see a doctor and find out if he was losing his mind. He had trouble keeping alert at times, and out here, with fifteen or so Pawnee just itching to take his scalp, that probably wasn't a good thing.

"Ya okay?" Uzziah asked.

See, even Uzziah could tell, something wasn't right about how his partner was acting.

"Yeah, okay," he said in a lackluster sort of way.

"Ya thirsty? I got plenty in my canteen." Uzziah held up the canteen.

"Nah." That was the other thing, it was getting hotter, Indian summer most likely, but tomorrow if it was really hot, then they would be through their water pronto, and heck, that didn't even count the horses, who were tied up back where there was plenty of prairie grass, and that had water in it, true, but they would need some, if not most, of the water that he and Uzziah had. Damn! This was getting to be a real pain in the arse!

———

No more Injuns tried crawling toward them, if in fact that was a Pawnee. Maybe Uzziah just shot a critter who was trying to get home, who knew? Well, they did know by sunrise, because there was a bloating body with a big knife between his teeth, damn savage!

By afternoon, the water was gone. Uzziah had foregone his share and given it to Shadow, and Immanuel couldn't blame him because if push came to shove, he could outride those Pawnee on a well-watered horse.

"This ain't lookin' good, Uzziah," Immanuel said, his lips parched and cracking.

"Things can change," Uzziah said in his inimitable way, always thinking positive thoughts.

"Things can stay the same, partner, they surely can."

"Maybe?"

"Ain't no maybe about the water. Look, I think ya should go fer help," Immanuel said, and Uzziah just laughed, he laughed so hard, he dropped his Hawken, and laughed some more as he picked it up.

"What's so funny?" Immanuel asked, his tongue sticking to the roof of his mouth.

"Help?" was all Uzziah said.

"Hey, wouldn't be the first time I've been left, maybe not the last," Immanuel said mysteriously.

"What the hell is that supposed to mean?"

"Nothin'," Immanuel said. "Just nothin'."

"I ain't ever left ya—"

"'Cept in that grave," Immanuel said and looked askance at Uzziah.

"But I came back," Uzziah said. "I came back."

"I know ya did, partner, and you will never know what a blessin' that was to me," Immanuel said. "But seriously, ride out and maybe enough of them'll foller ya that I can deal with the rest."

Uzziah looked at Immanuel. After all they'd been through, he wasn't about to leave the man to a certain death. Who would do that sort of thing? Not Uzziah.

———

For the next few days, things did not get better. Both men's lips were split and bleeding. Their thirst, well, it had gone beyond being thirsty to a sort of wish for the blessed drop of water—just one drop—to be left upon their tongues.

Every once in a while, one of them would rise up and fire a shot with their Hawken, which was generally greeted by shouts of execration. Well, they figured that's what they were since they didn't speak Pawnee. Immanuel figured he had come up with a viable solution.

"Tomorrow mornin' when them lazy ass Pawnee are just gettin' up, I'm gonna kill as many as I can."

"I'll go, too," Uzziah whispered, because it was all he could do to get out a sound. "We're ridin' right?"

"If the hosses will take us."

———

That night, as they lay nearly unconscious beside each other, Immanuel chuckled.

"Somethin' funny?" Uzziah asked.

"I been left afore, and I have been holdin' on to that day fer a long time."

"Who left ya?"

"My five brothers."

"But ya never…" Uzziah thought Immanuel had no brothers, and now he's finding out he had five of them?

"Hateful sons a bitches left me," Immanuel said.

"Where?"

"Up north way."

"Why?" Uzziah asked, realizing that if they weren't on the verge of their deaths, Immanuel would have gone to his grave with this family secret.

"As a sacrifice."

"What?"

"Ya deef? A sacrifice. We was like this, no food, no water, surrounded."

"How'd ya survive?"

"Funny story that."

"Tell me!"

"Sorry, young son, ain't got the breath, right now," Immanuel said, and his head sagged to one side and the man was asleep.

This revelation, and that's what it was, was just so disconcerting to Uzziah to know now that his partner had had five brothers, and he had thought and been led to believe that his family was best forgotten. No wonder. Uzziah wanted to shake Immanuel and get him to tell the rest of the story, but hell, he didn't have the strength to shake his own Johnson, not that he had anything left to piss out of it.

———

The next morning, with their stomachs pushing against their backbones, they checked the horses, and they were actually faring better than themselves.

They saddled up, well, they tightened the cinches on Trevor and Shadow, they needed tightening since the horses' midsections had diminished greatly. Immanuel looked at Uzziah over Trevor and saw how weak his partner was, and he felt about the same. Hell of a thing to ride into a suicide just to avoid the inevitable, well, it had been a good run, that's all Immanuel could think. Uzziah was muttering beside Shadow's head, and Immanuel thought he might be trying to talk to him.

"Ya talkin' to me?"

Uzziah shook his head and kept on muttering, then he whispered, "To Father."

Well, that there was the greatest difference between the two men. Uzziah believed that God was listening, and Immanuel sort of thought God had made the world and walked away. He'd heard that referred to as *the clockmaker. God* makes it, winds it up, and goes to lunch. Well, he wasn't talking to a God who had left and wasn't in the shop, he'd kill his last Injun—a Pawnee as it turned out. He often wondered what tribe the last Injun he killed was going to be from, now he knew, and that there was something anyway.

Then they heard some awful screaming. It didn't sound like the Pawnee because it wasn't. Another prairie tribe, the Lakota Sioux, had stumbled upon the camping Pawnee, and this was the party they were throwing for them.

They looked over the top of the boulders they were behind, and it was a pure dee massacre.

"Come on," Immanuel said as he led Trevor from their hideout and headed for the stream that they could hear the whole time but couldn't get close to. Uzziah followed him, and it was probably their total nonchalance about leaving and walking over to the stream that made them invisible to both the Pawnee and the Sioux.

There were boluses of water continuing to travel down both their horses' throats as they lay next to the stream and drank their fill. Immanuel looked up when a particularly gruesome scream cut through the morning air, and he saw, between the branches of the trees that were growing next to the stream, a Sioux pulling the entire scalp off a Pawnee's head. *Well, he wouldn't be needing it once he was dead*, Immanuel thought, then he reckoned that it would be best that they got out of this vicinity before there were no more Pawnee to carve on.

He nudged Uzziah, whose entire head was in the stream. "Huh?" Uzziah said.

Immanuel jerked his head away from the battle that was raging, and the two men led their mounts down the prairie until they mounted up and continued on the way.

———

That night, after they'd put a lot of distance between themselves and the fight that the Sioux had taken to the Pawnee, they stopped again beside a stream, and

Immanuel went to gathering wood for the cooking fire. When he came back, Uzziah was down by the stream just sitting by it. Immanuel strolled on over and looked down at his partner, who was sitting as quietly as if he were asleep, but his eyes were wide open.

Immanuel sat down beside Uzziah, and the two of them listened to the sound of the stream as it riffled its way across and over the rocks and pooled in certain areas, and went on down to wherever it was going.

It sounded like what the Bible called *a peace that passes all understanding*. That's the way it felt to Uzziah. Father had put a goat in the brambles, and they had been spared. They were not the ones laid upon the sacrificial altar, but those who had raised the knife against them, they had been sacrificed. Uzziah had come down to the stream to gather water for the grits, and after he'd filled the pot, he became mesmerized by the babbling of the brook. It was the voice of God, he was sure, and he needed to know exactly what God expected of him and his partner. They had been spared for a reason, and the reason was in the sound of the waters. He thought of Abooksigun up there in the area of the Yellow Rock River and his listening to the mud pots and finding meaning.

Neither man looked at the other as they sat and watched the last of the sun disappear and the colors of the setting orb fade to black. Finally, the horses, who had been grazing on prairie grasses, came over and stood behind each of their riders. They snorted softly, but made no more noises.

If anyone had wandered upon these four living creatures, they might have thought that some ritual was going on, but all that was going on was the beating of four hearts, the breathing of four sets of lungs, and the minds of each of the critters sailing away to a place where God listens and sometimes speaks.

Uzziah couldn't help but think of the second chapter of Philippians, where he had memorized these verses, *Let the same mind be in you that was in Christ Jesus, who though he was in the form of God, did not regard equality with God as something to be exploited, but emptied himself, taking the form of a slave, being born in human likeness. And being found in human form, he humbled himself and became obedient to the point of death—even death on a cross.*

Finally, Immanuel took the pot of water, built up the fire, and started the water to boil.

Uzziah thought that he could have stayed right there for eternity, but the idea of water with corn grits in it, and he could hear the bacon sizzling, well, his mind didn't lose the peace, but as he walked back to where Immanuel was cooking his dinner, he realized he would never be the same. Something had been given up back there when they were waiting for death, and his pleas for their lives had been answered, and he was so grateful. He looked at Immanuel, who smiled as he turned the bacon.

"Yer God came through, buddy."

"Our God."

"Yeah, well, I wasn't prayin' back there, but he musta heard ya."

"He did, and now, we are obliged."

"How's that?" Immanuel asked as he stirred the can of beans. "Ain't gonna be no biscuits, but hey," he said and shrugged.

"We're obliged to follow through," Uzziah said,

accepting the tin plate with the beans, bacon, and grits slouched over the sides.

"Follow through?" Immanuel said, taking a huge hot bite and shifting it around in his mouth to keep from getting burned too badly.

"On what ya told me, back there."

"What d'ya mean?'

"Immanuel, this meal is so good, it's been a long, long time since ya cooked for the both of us."

"Well, don't get all misty on me," Immanuel said, chuckling.

"When ya was a sacrifice, left by yer five brothers."

Immanuel put his plate down and added more beans. "Should never have told ya that, sorry."

"But ya did, old son, ya did."

"Reckon so, but if death hadn't been staring us both in the face, ya never woulda heard, never."

"But it was, and I did."

"Let's eat, then, while we smoke, I'll tell all," Immanuel said.

It was odd that you could live with someone, know them, you thought intimately, and still not know them. Uzziah tried not to rush through his plate of food, and he did take extra, well, they had starved with no way to cook, no water, yeah, they had jerked meat, but try eating that stuff with nothing to wash it down, not even spit!

Finally, they finished, and since Immanuel had cooked, Uzziah took the plates and such down by the stream and cleaned them Injun style with sand. When he came back, Immanuel was smoking, and Uzziah lit up, and they settled back on their bedrolls.

"Ya ain't gonna let this go, is ya?" Immanuel asked.

"Nope."

"My ma was a Mandan Injun. My pa was a White man, probably from the Lewis and Clarke expedition back in '04-'06. Nearest I can place my birthday is somewhere in there, probably '05, after they left the Mandan village and had built the fort. They stayed there that winter. Ma was a Mandan squaw, whose husband had died, but not afore givin' her five sons. She was well respected in the village, and raised up because of all the braves she gave the tribe."

"This the same Mandan village where we got the raft for the pelts?"

"Nah, the fort used to be there, but ma's tribal leanings are further west and north. She had been down to where they built the fort, but her people are in another section of the Mandan people, okay?"

"Well, I just wondered why we never visited her and yer brothers?"

"Young son, they left me, that's why."

"So, what happened?

"We was on a hunt, I was the youngest and not like my brothers, they all looked Injun I guess I resembled my pa, but I never met the man, nor do I know his name, don't matter. Anywho, this hunt was happenin'. We'd been follerin' this buffalo herd for days, and doin' all right, but it made us blind to whatever else was happenin' 'round us."

"Just you, yer ma, and yer five brothers?"

"Just the eight of us, anyway, one of the Assiniboine tribes—"

"The Sioux?"

"Yeah, the Sioux, the same tribe or one of their other tribes that just saved our bacon without them knowing it. Ya wanna hear this, or ya gonna keep interruptin'?"

Uzziah just looked at Immanuel and sat there all quiet-like.

"Okay, these Sioux, they was follerin' the herd, too. But we didn't know it till it was too late. There was a lot more of them than there was us, and we was basically surrounded, trapped just like back there, that's when my ma, she approached me. She said, 'Son,' I could speak fluent Mandan back then, galls me to speak it now, as ya know. She said, 'Son, we are sneaking away, but you must stay and keep firing arrows at the Sioux until ya have run out of them.' Can ya imagine how I felt? Don't answer that. I felt like she was sacrificing me 'cause I was half White, and she wanted to save her real sons, her red sons a bitches, the sons of her true husband."

"So, what did ya say to her?"

"Goodbye."

"Really?"

"What was I supposed to say? I had been brought up as a Mandan brave, and it was always our duty to protect home and family. If I hadn't stayed, they would have killed my brothers, taken my mother as a whore, and who knows what would have happened to me?"

"But the Sioux didn't kill ya?"

"Obviously, they thought it was funny that an Injun had a beard—yeah, at twelve years of age I had a bit of a beard and looked like a White man and all, but I had nothin' but a breech cloth and moccasins on, and I fought like hell when they overran me."

"So, ya was raised as a Sioux?"

"Hell no, they're a bunch of rabid dogs, and as soon

27

as the opportunity arose, I escaped and never looked back."

"Why didn't ya go back to yer Mandan family?"

"Those backstabbers, hell no! Again, they left me fer dead, and as far as they knew, I died back there, bunch of no-good red sons a bitches."

3

They rode for the next few days without much being said. Uzziah guessed correctly that the subject which his partner, Immanuel, had broached when they thought they were done for, was a subject he wished he'd have kept to himself. But Uzziah, being Uzziah, could not let the subject go. He just couldn't. The man had a family, and yes, they had done him wrong, perhaps even worse than wrong. It was a betrayal, for sure, but still, family was family, even if they were Mandans and his pa was some guy with Lewis and Clarke.

"Ya know, yer pa's most likely someone famous, now," Uzziah said as they were riding abreast.

Immanuel looked at Uzziah as if suddenly someone was riding with him that he didn't know.

"All those fellas made it back, except for that one guy who died fairly early. But yer pa, he's probably still alive."

"And this *pa* yer talkin' 'bout, I'm just sure he had all kinda soft and wonderful feelings fer me, don't ya think?" Immanuel was being his sarcastic self, and Uzziah knew the way around that.

"Well, yes, he probably does, probably has been searchin' fer ya fer years."

"Look, I knows ya was born yesterday, but—"

"Not yesterday mornin', not like I ain't heard that one before."

"Uzziah, you are not the same kinda man as me. Ya have a family, I've met yer family, and they are terrific, and I can see why ya would think that everybody's got that kinda family, but hear me when I say this, they don't"

"Yer poor ma has been mournin' ya since ya was overrun by the Sioux, and I wouldn't doubt it, ifn she didn't have a little shrine in her teepee, to ya."

Immanuel just looked at Uzziah like maybe, just maybe, he was stark raving mad.

"Yer brothers, now, I know they's feelin' guilt, such bad guilt, that they probably are half the men they would be if only they knew ya had made it through the ordeal," Uzziah said, really laying it on.

"My brothers have thought more about a good shite they had last week, than they have ever thought of me. Their guilt is non-existent, and it ain't the Injun way, anyways."

"How would ya know ya ain't really Mandan, are ya? Yer some mixture of an explorer and a woman who found comfort in his arms."

"Accent on the *com* part. My ma saw someone who was unusual, and to her, he was probably some hero-like guy. A White man who had come all the way out there, and she was sure she'd never see him again, so she did what any woman woulda done, she got herself a free lay. 'Cept it weren't free, his jism made her in a family way, and voilà! I was born. Not Mandan, not White, but a mixture that don't belong in any culture!"

"Maybe that's why ya drink so much?" Uzziah speculated openly.

"Ifn I had married a Mormon woman, I would expect this kinda shite comin' from her mouth, but young son, ya was born in Virginia, and yer family's got heads on their shoulders, and really, I expect ya to be more a man than ya sometimes are."

"So I'm being judged," Uzziah said and looked away.

"Oh my God, ifn I hadn't seen yer little ding-a-ling peeking out from that bush ya got down there, I don't know, Uzziah, I would be thinkin' 'bout now, that ya really are a damned woman!"

"Judgment, more judgment. Yer this way 'cause ya harbor hate in yer heart," Uzziah said.

"Yeah, I do, and I am about to unleash that hate on yer head, ifn ya don't stop this haranguing."

"A tragedy, that's what it is, a purdee tragedy just like Shakespeare would write. I can see the billboards now. Immanuel—the tragedy—don't let the name fool ya, he ain't with God, he's with the adversary!"

Yer steppin' on the Bard's toes, now, and none too kindly. He'd never touch my story and ya know it."

"Because it only has the first four acts, there remains a fifth act—the act of contrition, the act of humiliation, the act of forgiveness—"

That's all Uzziah got out before Immanuel leaped from Trevor and, grabbing Uzziah, took him to the ground. They rolled around a bit, and then Immanuel was on top of Uzziah, beating him in the face. Uzziah had his arms crossed and was blocking most of the blows and still talking!

"The onliest reason...yer treatin' yer partner...like this...is the great sadness yer carryin' in yer heart!" Uzziah said in between blows aimed at his face.

Finally, Immanuel lost all his strength as his blows became less than effective through his laughter. Immanuel rolled off Uzziah, and the laughter that came from the big man was contagious. Uzziah started laughing too.

"Okay, okay, okay, I give! Whatcha want me to do to git ya talkin' about somethin', anythin' else?" Immanuel asked as he rolled to a sitting position. Trevor came over and smelled him and snorted. "Trevor feels the same way, just tell me, old friend, and I swear I'll do it."

"Ya swear," Uzziah said, sitting up.

"I said it, I mean it."

———

They were riding up to a wood station on the Missouri. They could see the smoke from the paddle wheeler south and east of them. It would be there in about half an hour. Immanuel got off Trevor and watered him in the Missouri, and Uzziah simply sat on Shadow.

"I don't think this is a good idea," Uzziah said nervously.

"Ya want me to go see me family, yes?"

"Well, yeah."

"Then, this is the way we're gonna do it. We ain't ridin' the entire way when we can ride, more or less in luxury."

"But—"

"Ain't no buts 'bout it, either yer comin' with me, or ya gonna miss the return of the prodigal son."

"But last time we was on a paddle wheeler—"

"Don't say it, don't even think it, that was Uzziah and Immanuel, we ain't them. They're wanted by the Pinkertons fer the murder of Pinkerton Agent Robert Spells, and afore that the murder of an undersheriff in St. Louis—get it through yer head, they ain't us."

"Then, who are we?"

"We're brothers from Kentucky. I'm Horace Mann and yer my younger brother Archibald, but I calls ya Archie, ya got it?"

"I hate that name!"

"Then go onboard as Uzziah Ferguson O'Bannon and do enjoy yer hangin', that's what I say!"

Uzziah looked downstream and the paddle boat was getting closer. It would pull in at this wood station and load up. Immanuel got down into the wood that was there and was busy cutting it up in sizes that would fit into the boiler of the paddle wheeler.

"But what ifn they got dodgers on us?!?"

"What's they gonna look like, huh? Two big guys with big beards, jeez, that only describes every man this side of the Continental Divide, don't it?"

"But what if that Pinkerton lady—"

"Oh my God, Uzziah, worry should be yer middle name, ain't no Kate Warne gonna be on this chere paddle wheeler, she's back in Chicago climbing in and out of the bed of Alan Pinkerton."

"What about the captain?"

"There's probably close to fifty steam paddles on

the Missouri. What are the chances we get the same captain?"

"There's a two percent chance, Immanuel, two percent."

"Get down off Shadow and look like yer choppin' we might get our passage cut some ifn we look like we're workin', come on!"

Uzziah got down, and Shadow walked into the Missouri and drank while Uzziah picked up an axe and started chopping. Immanuel bent down and threw some water on himself and Uzziah.

"What the hell?"

"Gots ta look like we been sweatin', fool," Immanuel said as they heard the steam whistle blow. They were coming into the wood station.

It was fairly common for White folks to get passage in this way. If you knew the times and waited at a wood station, you could purchase passage as far up as ya wanted to go.

The sailors threw their lines over the moorings and then got off to start throwing the wood on board.

"We'll throw it up, ya put it away, what d'ya say?" Immanuel asked the two sailors who had gotten off. They agreed, and he and Uzziah threw the wood up and were standing next to the boiler room when the captain came down and was observing them.

"Ya want passage?"

"We do," Immanuel answered, Uzziah being too shy to look at the man, thinking well, there was a two percent chance!

"How far?"

"Mandan Fort," Immanuel said.

"Ya workin' it off, or ya got money?"

"Workin' ifn ya don't mind?" Immanuel asked.

"Sleepin' on the main deck, that's what ya'll be doin'," the captain said.

"Fine with us," Immanuel said.

"What's yer names, lads?"

"I'm Horace Mann, this chere's my brother Archie," Immanuel said, pointing to Uzziah, who just kept throwing wood and not looking up.

"Is he a deaf/mute?"

"Archie, speak to the captain."

"Thank ye, captain, fer allowin' us onboard," Uzziah said, and kept right on throwing wood.

"He's a polite one, ain't he," the captain said.

"Ma's favorite, she spoiled him and he's a bit shy, misses her terrible-like, could say he were a mama's boy," Immanuel said, and Uzziah gave him a look.

"Don't play with that. I'm such and proud of it!" the captain said as he took the stairs up to the pilot house.

"See what ya get when ya go too fer?" Uzziah said.

"What kinda man admits he's a mama's boy?"

"The kind that pilots this chere vessel?"

———

They got situated on board, put Trevor and Shadow in the stable, and paid the man who fed them.

"If this un causes ya any trouble, come and git me," Uzziah said, referring to Shadow.

The man was as old as Immanuel and his eyes were rummy. "He ain't gonna cause me nothin' but pleasure. Just lookin' at him is enough to make a man smile."

"Well, still, call me ifn there's anything unusual," Uzziah said.

"I can see somebody's got them a good rider who appreciates a good horse."

Uzziah flipped the man a little extra just in case.

It was growing evening, and as the sun began to set, Immanuel pushed his bedroll up against the wall that separated the main deck from the boiler room.

"Put yer roll up chere, Archie," Immanuel said. "It's warmer."

Of course, they could take the stairs to the boiler deck. Most passengers had their rooms there, and there was a saloon—just one—on this particular paddle wheeler, all of them were different in some way. They sauntered on up to the saloon and bellied up to the bar. The barkeep looked them over and pointed to the bar top. He wanted to see money before he served them. Immanuel placed a couple of silver dollars on the bar, and Uzziah looked at him oddly.

"Always gots to have a reserve, young son," Immanuel said.

They were gladly given a whiskey each, and Immanuel took the change over to one of the tables where there was a poker game.

"Got room fer one more?" Immanuel asked. There were only three at the table.

"More than welcome, more than welcome!" said the man who looked like he was a professional gambler, and had the majority of chips sitting in front of where he sat. The other two were an older gentleman who looked like he might be a drummer, and a rather young man, who had a whisp of a mustache and was dressed too well for the west.

There were introductions made all around, and Uzziah stayed away from the table since some men used other men to signal what was in the other player's hands. The kitty was filled, and Immanuel made a modest bet and lost. Uzziah turned away, whatever reserve Immanuel had, Uzziah was sure he was going to lose it in the next hour.

Uzziah walked out on the boiler deck, sat in a chair, and watched the moon rise. He was enjoying the whiskey, it wasn't too watered down, and with the moon reflecting on the Missouri, he felt like he was back on the other ship, when Kate Warne had seduced him into telling her his real name and all that trouble started. There did seem to be someone sitting away from him and to his right, and they were in the shadows. He turned and looked at them, and it was a young couple who were stealing kisses in the darkness. That was nice to see. Perhaps Immanuel had been right? What was he thinking? Of course he was right. There was nothing to be afraid of with all the paddle wheelers on the Missouri, their luck would have to be extraordinarily bad for them to end up on the same ship.

"How long you and yer brother been out this way?" It was the captain, and he sat down next to Uzziah.

"He came out afore me, but I guess we been trappin' and stayin' up in the mountains together fer a while, why?"

"Ya fit the description of two hombres that wrecked another pilot's boat. I don't care if ya are them, I just don't want any trouble, ya understand. What ya say yer name was again?"

"Archibald Witherspoon Mann," Uzziah said, adding the middle name made it seem more realistic.

"I knew some Wetherspoons down Tennesssee way, ya from there?"

"No, we're from the hills of Kentucky, the place ain't got a proper name yet," Uzziah said.

"Just wonderin'. Say, we been havin' some trouble with Injuns shootin' arrows at the boats lately. Probably some damned young brave's idea of havin' fun. You and yer brother, what's his name?"

"Horace," Uzziah said.

"Yeah, ifn ya chime in with those big rifles like the ⟩ who wrecked that paddle wheeler of my friend's, hen and if the Injuns show up, I'll give ya a dollar a piece fer each one ya knock from the saddle, but I didn't say that. There's so many damned Nancies runnin' around and people worrying about the all-fired Injun like he was somethin' to worry 'bout. Just tally up yer score when—and like I said, if—the show begins, and I'll pay ya outta my own pocket. The last thing we need is folks being scared to ride the Mighty Mo. Okay, nice chattin' with ya," the captain said and walked off nonchalant-like.

Uzziah went back into the saloon and Immanuel must have been on a winning streak because he had a large stack of chips and a smile a mile wide on his face. He handed Uzziah a few chips to cash in, and Uzziah got Immanuel another whiskey and himself one, too.

The man who looked like the professional gambler was wearing his poker face in a frown. Maybe he always looked like that, but Uzziah didn't think so. The fella with the pencil-thin mustache was smiling, and Uzziah guessed he was happy Immanuel was winning and not the other guy.

They ordered roast beef sandwiches with horse-radish from the galley, and Immanuel ate his at the poker table to a disgruntled professional player, who spoke up about it.

"It ain't proper to eat at the card table," the man said.

"Well, to hell with proper, do you other gentlemen object?"

"Fine by me," the drummer said, and ordered a sandwich for himself.

"What about you, young man, you look like ya got a proper upbringing, can he eat at the poker table?" the professional gambler asked.

"Well, he's been eating yer winnings since he got here, seems to me ya outta be glad he's got an appetite fer something besides yer money," the young man said to everyone's astonishment.

"Thank ye," Immanuel said, and was thinking he wasn't sure who this young fella was, but it was obvious he had an education and he knew how to use words. Immanuel believed the professional gambler was sorry he asked all around the table for their opines.

Also, Immanuel was aware of when the man, who considered himself a professional gambler, was dealing from the bottom of the deck and when he would throw in his hand and not bet much. The man was a cheat, and not a bad one, but Immanuel had seen better. If this was in a saloon, on the prairie, Immanuel would have put a hole through this professional's chest, but he was having such luck with the man cheating like he was, he thought he'd just let it go for now.

Finally, the young man, his name was Austin

Fielder, began seeing when Immanuel would throw his cards in, and he was beginning to follow suit. The only one who didn't know the professional gambler was cheating was the drummer, and he seemed okay with giving the man his money.

4

By the time Immanuel and Uzziah rolled into their bedrolls, Immanuel had pretty well taken all the pro's monies from him. He saw the man talking to the captain, and the captain just looked over and dismissed whatever the man was saying and walked away. Immanuel was fairly sure that he had been accused of cheating. The pro probably couldn't have figured any other way for a backwoodsman—he'd actually used that term in relation to Uzziah and Immanuel —how someone from the back woods could have taken him for such a loss.

The young man, Austin Fielder, bought Uzziah and Immanuel both a drink before they settled down on the main deck to sleep, and he had some interesting conversation for a youngster.

"So, you two are mountain men?" Austin asked right after they'd settled down at one of the tables away from the gambling, having a nice view of the moonlit Missouri drifting by.

"Yes, we are," Uzziah said, not afraid of someone of so obvious a young age.

"I heard this story when I was back in St. Louis—"

"Is that where yer from?" Immanuel asked him.

"No, no, I come from Camden, New Jersey, sort of a garden spot in the Garden State.

"Never been there," Immanuel said.

"And you probably never will!" Austin said and laughed for no particular reason.

"Whatcha do fer a livin'?" Uzziah asked, seeing that he was so young and out here on the Missouri all by himself.

"I'm a journalist," Austin said.

"What's a journalist?" Immanuel asked.

"Yeah, we ain't ever heard of no such job," Uzziah chimed in.

"I write for newspapers, different ones. They call me a stringer, 'cause I write fer different papers, and if they want the story I write, they pick it up and I make some money."

"Is there good money in writing?" Immanuel always went to the bottom line.

"Well, some, but most of that I would have lost at the table tonight if it hadn't been fer you, sir," he said and he raised his glass in a toast.

Immanuel and Uzziah raised theirs.

"He was cheating, wasn't he?" Austin asked.

"Yeah, he weren't too good at it, and I didn't feel like killin' him," Immanuel said.

"But in another place and time?" Austin suggested excitedly.

"Heavens yes," Uzziah said. "This man does not like cheaters."

Immanuel just smiled.

"I'm following a story, maybe you two can help me with it?"

"Do we get paid to help ya with it?" Immanuel asked, smiling, and Austin looked discouraged.

"Only kiddin', kid. What ya need to know? We can help ya out, I'm sure," Immanuel said, and Uzziah realized he, Immanuel, was getting into his cups and one misspoke word and their cover would be blown.

"I'm following these two mountain men, much like yerslves. Their names are Uzziah Ferguson O'Bannon and Immanuel James Jones. Have ya heard of them?"

Both mountain men looked at each other, but it was only a look.

"Maybe a whisper," Immanuel said, winking at Uzziah, who hoped the kid didn't pick up on the wink.

"Well, they were wanted for killing an undersheriff in St. Louis, then they killed a Pinkerton agent by the name of Robert Spells. The last they were heard of, they outfoxed a very successful Pinkerton agent who was a woman. I know it's hard to believe, but you can't make this stuff up." Austin paused as he sipped his whiskey, he wasn't exactly a big drinker.

Uzziah and Immanuel exchanged concerned glances, but Immanuel was smiling like he was going to mess with the boy. Uzziah certainly hoped that wasn't the case.

"Anyway, on a paddle wheeler just like this one, the female agent, her name was Kate Warne, she got the drop on these two. The older one, and I'm assuming the wiser, jumped off the ship, or so they thought. She took the younger one for some questioning, but somehow the older one, who had jumped off the paddle wheeler, was still on it, and he burst through the door guns blazing, took his partner back, and they escaped. But here's the really good part. Since they were traveling to St. Louis, they laid out on the prairie and disabled the paddle wheeler by shooting off the wheel and disabling it in the middle of the stream. Can ya beat that?" he said and swigged the rest of his whiskey and started coughing.

Immanuel slapped him on the back so he could get his breath back.

"Thank you."

"That sounds like one of them—what d'ya call it, Archie? One of them tall tales, that's what that sounds like to me, Mr. Austin Fielder. It sure does, s'pose ya might be chasin' a shadow of the real story," Immanuel said.

Uzziah, meantime, had his glass half frozen to his mouth and was simply holding it there. Immanuel kicked him under the table, and Uzziah finally took a drink.

"Tell me, Archie, do all mountain men carry those Hawken rifles like you guys have with you all the time?"

Uzziah looked like a deer caught in the shunted lantern light, then he finally spoke.

"That's a good question, Austin. No, they don't. We carry them because of their firepower and their range. A lot of mountain men have gone to newer, and in my opinion, less reliable armaments," Uzziah said and wondered why he said armaments, they were rifles, simple as that.

"What about you, Horace?" Austin asked Immanuel, who was looking off at the Missouri, it was captivating.

"Horace, Horace, the man asked ya a question,"

Uzziah said. "Ya'll have to forgive him—he's lot older than me, and he's losing his hearin'."

"Oh, I'm sorry," Austin said, speaking way too loud for someone at the same table. "Can you hear me now?" he veritably yelled.

"Archie likes to jest, I ain't hard of hearin' I was just admirin' the Mighty Mo," Immanuel said.

"Why do you carry the Hawken?" Austin asked Immanuel.

"Well, my partner there has told me that the captain of this very ship has asked us to help out. It seems we're about to enter a section of the river where Injun braves are shooting arrows at the paddle wheelers just fer the fun of it. He's asked us to shoot back, but not fer fun. Ifn that happens, ya'll see why we favor the Hawken. Thank ye, fer the drink, but we must be gettin' our beauty sleep," Immanuel said, and Uzziah couldn't have been any happier.

———

Now, snuggled against the warm wall which separated the boiler room from the boiler deck, Uzziah was anxious to hear just what he thought about Austin's story.

"We're famous," Immanuel said.

"It's called infamous," Uzziah corrected him.

"And fer all the wrong reasons. Ya know, I'd like to tell that there fella the true story of Immanuel and Uzziah."

"Ya mean the true story of Uzziah and Immanuel," Uzziah corrected.

"People think we're bad men, bad hombres, but we

been standin' up fer what is right and true fer the longest time, young son," Immanuel said.

"And ya think tellin' a journalist—still can't believe that's a job—our story, and yer thinkin' it wouldn't get twisted 'round like everythin' that ever happened to us?" Uzziah asked.

"I don't know, he seemed honest to me," Immanuel said.

"And may I remind ya, yer drunk."

"Yeah, I know, got that glow wishin' I was with a gal, but still, even with this glow on, he seemed an original, ya know, like he might be worth tellin' the whole story to."

"Are ya gonna give him directions to the cabins?"

Immanuel just looked at Uzziah.

"I think I liked ya better as Archie," Immanuel said and turned over and, with the astonishing speed of a man falling off a cliff, was asleep.

———

The morning broke like no other had ever broken. Uzziah was having a dream, and in the dream, there were Injuns shooting arrows at him and Immanuel, and they were just ignoring them. Then there was a loud clunk just above his head, and, awakening and looking up, there was a flaming arrow stuck into the side of the boiler room. Immanuel had already grabbed his Hawken, which was never more than arm's distance away, and every time it wasn't, something bad had happened to them.

The passengers were hiding in their cabins, and the

crew was running around trying to extinguish the flaming arrows.

"It's the damn Sioux, one minute they're saving our lives, the next minute they're tryin' to kill us. Notionality at its best!" Immanuel said as he sighted down the Hawken. Tricky shot this, a moving boat, Sioux on horses riding downstream with the direction of the water, and away from the direction of the boat.

BOOM! Immanuel's Hawken exploded, and not one, but two Sioux, the one riding opposite the one shooting arrows, maybe he was lighting them, who knew? But both were snatched off their ponies and thrown to the ground.

"That's what I'm talkin' 'bout," Immanuel said, reloading faster than any man alive.

Uzziah was lying down on the main deck and made a very small target, but arrows, flaming and otherwise, were still sticking to the main deck around him. He fired, and only one Sioux went down.

Running from the boiler deck down the stairs came Austin Fielder, with his pad and pencil. He licked the pencil and, hiding behind a barrel, he began writing feverishly.

"Ain't ya got a weapon, son?" Immanuel asked him.

"Haven't ya heard, Horace, the pen is mightier than the sword," Austin yelled. There was a lot of commotion on the paddle wheeler, and women in their staterooms were screaming as some smoke was filling their cabins. One woman ran from her smoky room only to be impaled by a flaming arrow. Her dress must have been made from some flammable material because she instantly burst into flames and ran the length of the paddle wheeler, the crew running after her, till she tripped over the balustrades of the railing and fell to the main deck below, right beside Austin Fielder, who immediately threw up.

Immanuel grabbed a burlap sack and beat the flames out, but the woman was, thankfully, dead.

They continued firing and reloading, and firing and reloading until it became obvious to the Sioux that it was a losing battle. The Sioux didn't want the paddle wheelers going up the Missouri and taking White men with it, so they're recourse was to make the journeys as harrowing for the passengers as possible.

But that was the way a White man would look at it. The smell of bar-b-que filled the main deck.

The Sioux pulled away from the Missouri and fell to a position that they thought was out of range for the White man's rifles.

"Them stupid bastards think they's out of range, Uzziah! Let's show 'em what we got, young son," Immanuel said, and he had used his partner's name without even thinking about it.

Behind the barrel, and still writing furiously, Austin Fielder heard what Immanuel had said. He had called his partner, Uzziah, he had! That meant that these two men were precisely the men he had been hearing about, and no matter what they called themselves, they were the real McCoy's! He had just struck journalistic gold!

Maybe Uzziah hadn't noticed what Immanuel had called him, besides, what was more natural than being called by your real name?

They loaded up and adjusted their sights for long range, and lying very still, they breathed in and out, in and out, then both Hawkens exploded at the same time, and Austin Fielder looked to where the Sioux sat comfortably on their horses and discussed the havoc they had produced, when two of them jerked slightly, well, at that range, he could barely see it, but they did jerk, then sluffed off their horses.

All the rest of the Sioux yipped it up and looked toward the paddle wheeler where Uzziah and Immanuel were busy reloading, lying on their sides, then they were down again, but not before the Sioux were headed further away. Still, it made no difference, as both mountain men's rifles threw fire from their muzzles, Austin took his opera glasses from his coat and looked down range. One, then a second Sioux, arched their backs and slumped over their ponies only to fall off as the ponies kept running.

"Amazing shots! Simply amazing shots!" Austin yelled, and the crew and passengers who had gathered on the deck above broke into a spontaneous applause for the two partners.

Immanuel got up and helped Uzziah up. They brushed their deerskins off and headed up to the saloon, where there was a line of men waiting and willing to buy them whiskey.

Immanuel stopped beside the barrel, which Austin was still crouched behind.

"By the by, ya might wanna be more careful 'bout the barrels ya hide behind," Immanuel said, and Austin looked at the side of the barrel, which was marked **TNT**. He scurried away from it as if it might explode after the fact, and Uzziah and Immanuel chuckled as they made their way up the stairs.

Austin fell back among all the gladhanders. He had something on his mind that was better than simply congratulating the two mountain men. What had they said their names were?—Horace and Archibald! He had to hand it to them, they had balls made from the best fired brass, which had driven all the dross from them. They had boarded another streamer just like the one they had disabled not less than a year ago. They were throwing everything in the face of the law and getting by with it.

It was then that Austin Fielder remembered the phrase, The wild, wild west! Yes, this was certainly what that meant. It was a territory where men made their own fates, where men did what needed to be done, and to hell with any consequences, and the more they did not shrink from what they had done, the bolder and braver they acted. It seemed this west, which was truly wild, was rewarding them.

He wanted to get the real story. There were always two sides, hell, sometimes there were a dozen sides to the same story, and he knew in his heart of hearts that their story had not been told. He, Austin Fielder, a stringer for the newspapers back east, would get the real tale, the honest story. And if these men were villains, then he would gladly paint them as such, but he had an idea that they had been demonized by the sensitivities of those back east who had taken on the veneer of a society that said, 'Bless you,' when a man sneezed and killed you with gossip behind the same man's back.

At least out here, these men did not make any qualms about who they were, well, sometimes aliases were necessary, but they acted on their instincts and relied on those same instincts to carry them through.

He had been writing this all this down as a sort of preamble to the piece he knew he could get from them when there was loud laughter, and when he looked up

Immanuel was grinning from ear to ear, and the one he called Archie, whom he now knew was Uzziah was laughing too and looking at his partner with a look which every man wished to have thrown his way. It was pure, unadulterated admiration and love. The two mountain men had bonded in their adventures and become what all men wished to be—companions of other real men!

———

As the party waned into the evening and the professional gambler had even bought the two mountain men drinks, Uzziah and Immanuel were eating a free dinner on the steamboat company for their help in riding this particular journey of loathsome Injuns, when the captain walked up.

"I knows we done got ya drunk, and are feedin' yer arses, but here's a little something which the company set aside for such heroism," he said and tossed a pouch full of clinking coins on the table between the two men and walked away. Both their eyes went to the sack and they smiled at each other.

"Can it get any better, partner?" Immanuel asked Uzziah.

"It's 'bout to get worse, I'm afeared," Uzziah said.

"What's ya talkin' 'bout?" Immanuel asked.

"During the melee and all the ruckus, ya called me by my Christian name," Uzziah whispered.

Immanuel just looked at Uzziah and frowned. "No, I did not."

"Partner, it was plain as day. And even though all hell was breaking loose 'round us and that there lady was still smolderin' and smellin' like real good bar-be-que, old Mr. Journalist, he heard, he certainly took note."

"Nah, yer just imaingin' things." Immanuel was tryin' to assure himself.

"I'm tellin' ya, he heard, I could see the understandin' in his face," Uzziah said.

"Shite," Immanuel said as he let his eyes go throughout the saloon till they landed on Austin Fielder, who was talking to some lady and writing stuff down. He was probably getting her hysterical account of what had happened and how it affected her. Austin looked up and, catching Immanuel's eye, smiled and went back to writing.

"He don't look like he knows," Immanuel said.

"That's how ya know he knows," Uzziah said.

"Crap, looks like we'll be makin' an early exit off this chere boat and ridin' the rest of the way to Mandan village," Immanuel said.

"Fine by me, I'm just glad there's no law on this bucket of bolts," Uzziah said.

———

At the next wood station, Uzziah saddled up Shadow and Trevor, who seemed to have been fed well. He gave the older man, who was in charge of the livestock, another coin, and he bit it, not believing it could be gold.

Immanuel came down and they put the bits in their horses' mouths.

"He see ya?" Uzziah asked.

"Nah, he's made hisself a friend of the lady whose friend got burned to death," Immanuel said.

"Good fer him," Uzziah said as they mounted up and waited for the boarding plank to be let down so the crew could gather wood. The minute it was down, they rode off and headed north.

"Excuse me," Austin said to his new companion.

"Certainly," she said, expecting him to return, but Austin Fielder went down and, having already saddled his horse, mounted up and ran it off the gangplank right before it was hoisted up.

The woman he'd been interviewing and who was certain that her comments would be read in the newspapers back home, looked out over the plains, and who should be hightailing it away north but Austin Fielder. *Well, the nerve of some people*, she mused, and thought no more of it.

5

Uzziah and Immanuel had kicked their horses up once they were out of sight of the river and made fairly good time. They took both Trevor and Shadow back to a dogtrot and were fairly happy they had avoided being called out on the steam vessel.

"How fer ya figure it to be?" Uzziah asked.

"Not fer, not fer at'all," Immanuel said. "Say, did we make out like bandits or what?"

"Got plenty of gold, ifn that's what yer askin'," Uzziah said.

"Yeah, wish I'd been smart enough to convert some of that wealth into whiskey."

"Heavens, old son, the captain would have gladly given ya some of his bonded all ya had to do was ask." Uzziah grinned.

"Is that yer way of tellin' me that ya did that?"

"No, that's my way of tellin' ya I could have done that, ifn whiskey is that high on yer priority list."

"Who the hell has a priority list?" Immanuel spat out.

"Anybody who's got direction in their life."

"So, ya got one?"

"I do."

"Let me see it," Immanuel asked and held out his hand.

"It's a list, but it ain't printed," Uzziah explained.

"How can it be a list and not be printed out?"

"Simple, I gots me a mind."

"So, this supposed list it's in yer head?"

"It is."

"Let me hear it," Immanuel almost demanded.

"Why? It ain't yer list."

"Ah-ha! Ya ain't got one, same as me," Immanuel challenged Uzziah.

"No, no, I gots one, but it's my priority list, not yourn."

"Ain't got one, neither do I, knew it, just knew it," Immanuel taunted.

"Got one, as sure as there's a sun in the noonday sky, got one!"

"No, ya don't."

"I do!"

"If ya had one ya could recite it right off the top of yer head, 'cause it's what ya consider the most important, ain't that what priority means?"

"Yeah, so?"

"So, ifn ya had it in yer dang head there somethin' that ya considered most important in yer life, ya sure as hell be able to tell me what this so-called most important list is, and since ya can't tell me, ya don't have one, simple as that."

Uzziah looked at Immanuel and started listing, "The Bible, God's grace, Jesus Christ's death on the cross, the Holy Ghost, repentance, forgiveness, forgiving, righteousness, wisdom, and being happy."

Immanuel just looked at his partner with a slack mouth, then said, "Bet ya can't repeat that!"

"The Bible, God's grace, Jesus Christ's death on the cross, the Holy Ghost, repentance, forgiveness, forgiving, righteousness, wisdom, and being happy."

Immanuel looked away and looked back at Uzziah, who was simply riding Shadow and looking straight ahead.

They rode for a minute or two.

"So's ya got yerself a priority list?" Immanuel asked.

"I do, I do," Uzziah said, and the two men rode on as if nothing had happened.

———

Behind them, back a long way, Austin Fielder was watching them argue through his opera glasses. Actually, they were his dearly departed mother's opera glasses, and she did love it when men sang high notes. Her favorite opera, Mozart's ***The Marriage of Figaro***, to which she had taken her son on every occasion it had played at the opera house in Baltimore, Maryland.

He brought the glasses down and thought how ironic it was that he had seen tenors bursting their lungs and straining their balls in arias, and now he was watching probably the two most dangerous men on the earth. He would have rewritten that line, it was a bit melodramatic, and they were only dangerous, he had come to the conclusion, to those who got in their way.

He was lost in those thoughts when he rode through a copse of trees, and then, taking the glasses back up, looked up the trail again to see just how far he was from Immanuel James Jones and Uzziah Ferguson O'Bannon.

"Back c'here, scribbler." Immanuel's voice cut through Austin like a knife, and for a moment, he couldn't believe that they had gone from being so far in front of him to directly behind him. It had been his musings about his mother's love of opera that had distracted him. If he was killed, it would surely be her fault.

———

They took his weapon away, which was an antique, almost. It was the US Musket Charleville pattern, a 69-caliber flintlock musket.

"Where in the hell did ya git this?" Immanuel asked, admiring the old flintlock and handling it like it was a treasure.

"My pa, he was in the Army for a while," Austin said.

"No shite!" Uzziah said, taking the flintlock away from Immanuel and examining it.

"Ya coulda helped us the other day on the boat, this thing'll take out somethin' at three hundred yards, ifn yer a good shot," Immanuel said, then added, "Can ya shoot the dang thing?"

"Yeah, why else would I carry it?" Austin said.

"Let me see," Immanuel said, handing the musket back to Austin.

"Ya think that's a good idea?" Uzziah asked.

"Unless we line up with each other, he can only kill one of us, then reload."

"That's reassuring."

Austin got off his horse and handed the reins to Uzziah. "You mind?" he asked, and Uzziah nodded that he didn't.

"What you want me to shoot?" Austin looked up at Immanuel as he shielded his eyes from the sun.

"Ya see that there wad of whatever at the end of that limb about 100 yards away, sticking out over the trail?"

"Yeah, want me to shoot that?"

"Yeah."

Austin raised the musket up on the perpendicular to his body and opened up the pan, then he reached into his cartridge pouch and withdrew a paper cartridge and bit it open. He poured a portion of the powder into the pan and closed it. He poured the rest of the powder down the barrel, followed by the ball he was going to shoot, then paper that the powder was caught up in, then, taking the ramming rod, Austin rammed it down several times, until everything in the barrel was tightly packed. He put the ramrod back in its holder on the rifle, then he took the rifle from halfcocked to full cock, and brought the weapon up to his shoulder, sighting down the road toward the object which Immanuel had pointed out to him.

They could see him squeezing the trigger, and the pan flashed and the musket fired.

Immanuel had taken out his spyglass and was watching downrange.

"He got it!"

"He hit it?" Uzziah asked.

"Yeah, clean through, whatever it was is gone," Immanuel said, turning to Austin, "Who taught ya how to shoot, yer old man?"

"Of course, it was his musket."

"So, why didn't ya help us on the steamer?" Uzziah asked.

"Ya didn't need my help, ya did just fine the two of ya," Austin said, smiling. "Can I sling the musket back on my shoulder?"

"Depends, why are ya follerin' us?" Immanuel asked.

"Truth?"

"Of course, nothin' less will do," Uzziah said.

"I heard ya call yer partner by his real name—"

"I knew it!" Uzziah shouted.

"And?" Immanuel asked.

"I think I can clear both your names. I don't think you're murderers, and if you tell me your story, I can have it published, and who knows what will happen?"

————

They made the scribbler, as Immanuel called him, ride in front of them, and kept their eyes on him as they rode toward Mandan village. Austin got a crick in his neck from turning his head and talking to them, and all in all, it was an entertaining ride till sunset.

He even explained about the strange-looking opera

glasses with the extended arm for holding them up to the eyes. The magnification was weak, only three times, and he told them the original name of them, which was Galilean binoculars. He then went on to explain the plot of The Marriage of Figaro and sang them part of the tenor's aria.

When he was singing, he had to turn to the front, and Immanuel made crazy eyes at Uzziah during the singing, and Uzziah could almost not stop from laughing, but all in all, the boy, Austin, had a most wonderful voice, and since they didn't know anything about opera, they thought Austin's performance was amusing, if nothing else.

Austin tried explaining to them that the most interesting part of opera was that everyone could be talking —singing—at the same time, and it was their harmonies, even if they were at odds in the story of the opera, which made up the real music.

The two mountain men looked at each other as if it were being explained to them how things worked on the moon. They smiled a lot and nodded, which Austin thought would have made them great supernumeraries in an opera.

———

At dinner that night, after Uzziah had cooked, naturally, and they had had their fill of biscuits, rabbit, bacon, and beans, Immanuel poured coffee for them and handed out the tin mugs.

"Would you like something to make this Irish?" Austin asked.

Immanuel looked at Uzziah, who looked at Austin. "Does he mean?" Immanuel asked.

"I'm sure he does," Uzziah said.

Austin went to his saddlebags and pulled from it a bottle of Jameson whiskey, and you'd have thought that he was showing Immanuel one of the Holy Relics.

Immanuel examined the bottle, the wax seal had not been broken, and he handed it back to Austin.

"You don't want any?" Austin asked.

"Do us the honor," Immanuel said, and Austin broke the wax seal and poured their coffee full to the brim with the Irish whiskey.

After the third Irish coffee, they simply poured the whiskey directly into the tin cups and drank. When everyone seemed sufficiently lubricated, Austin spoke, "Please tell me what happened in St. Louis and how it came to be that Robert Spells was killed, and how, pray tell, did you get away not once, but twice from Kate Warne, the only female Pinkerton agent?"

A bit bleary-eyed, Immanuel looked at Uzziah, who graciously gestured with an open palm that Immanuel should hold forth.

Immanuel was like a squeezebox that only needed the energy of whiskey to pump him. He talked for close to three hours. Uzziah curled up in his bedroll and listened, but admittedly fell asleep before it was over.

What was amazing was that Austin Fielder never stopped writing in what he later admitted to them was shorthand. He showed them his notes, and it looked like a foreign language, but Austin swore that from those notes, he could retell the tale which Immanuel had told him word by word.

Immanuel started out with the murder of the undersheriff, for which he said he and Uzziah were willing to take credit, that was the word he used, credit for it. He told of the woman whose name they could not say and how they both loved her. The last trick of that woman to get the monies they needed to go back to the Rockies, how the undersheriff had slit her open, and they had snuck to the man's house in the middle of the night and taken him to the first wood station. Austin remembered someone aboard the steamer telling him that was where the undersheriff had been murdered.

But Immanuel went on to explain, they simply didn't just kill the man, they stripped every bit of skin off his body and left him for the wild animals. Austin's face was ghostly white as Immanuel went on to tell how Robert Spells, the greenhorn Pinkerton agent, had found them helping the wagon train to Oregon, and how they'd taken him back up the mountains and released him only to have him lose his way and freeze to death.

"Can we be blamed for a man's incompetence?!? And surely his incompetence does not equal us being murderers?" Immanuel shouted as if he were standing in front of a jury at his own trial.

At one point—Uzziah thought it might have been when they were with Abooksigun and they had ridden their horses into the lake, and the US Army and Kate Warne were behind them, and the fog came in over the lake—Immanuel was up in front of the fire, his arm gracefully sweeping the fog over the lake, and Uzziah could almost hear the whinnying of the horses as they rode into the cold lake, or was that Immanuel actually making those noises?

Then, later, Uzziah awakened, and Immanuel had collapsed beside the fire, and Austin had covered him with a blanket. Austin was reading his notes, and when he looked up and saw that Uzziah was looking at him, he spoke. "This story will captivate an audience and win you both your freedom, I'm certain of it," Austin said, then he sipped his whiskey, curled up in his bedroll, and fell asleep.

———

The young man who had followed them from the paddle boat steamer was awake by the time Uzziah was making biscuits and putting them in the Dutch oven. He jumped up out of his bedroll, ran behind a tree, and peed. Uzziah grinned to himself, thinking of Immanuel just standing up out of his bedroll and shooting his piss a bit further off than where he'd slept. The boy was modest, and that was fine by Uzziah.

"What are you making?" Austin asked as he came back and squatted by the fire with his hands sticking out toward it.

"Breakfast for the lot of us," Uzziah said, and wondered what the boy would do if he told him what he and his partner were up to. "Say, we're gonna go on to a Mandan village a bit north and west of the old Mandan Fort, would ya like to tag along?"

"Would I?!?"

"Yeah, that's what I'm askin', young son," Uzziah said and thought about how that was what Immanuel always called him, and now he could return the favor to someone else.

"Yes, I surely would."

"Good, now listen close before Immanuel wakes up from his whiskey sleep. When Lewis and Clark came through this area back in ought '4 through '8 weren't none of us alive, but one of his men put a Mandan woman in a family way," Uzziah started out, and the boy's hand slipped into his saddle bags and brought out the notebook he'd kept notes in the night before, and he began to scribble.

Whether it was right or wrong, Uzziah really didn't care, what he knew was that Immanuel was always thirsty for attention, and if this escapade of his life could be included with everything that Immanuel had told the journalist the night before, then, he, Uzziah, felt the chances that his partner might actually go through with it were greatly increased. Maybe he was queering the deal, but he thought not. He went through the entire story of his five other brothers and his ma being out hunting buffalo, and how the Sioux had come upon them, and it looked like they were about to be overrun when his brothers left him, and his ma right along with them.

"Is he going to kill the lot of them?" Austin asked.

Uzziah cut his eyes over to where Immanuel was still snoring, you can't fake a snore, then back at the boy.

"No, he is not."

"Why not? It sounds like something he might do." Austin asked.

"Yeah, it does, but he's been tormented by them leaving him—"

"Wouldn't that torment go away when he dispatched them all?"

"No, then their guilt would become his guilt. I know yer young, son, but try to think Biblically."

"Don't the Bible teach an eye for an eye?"

"No, not always. Try thinking of the story of Joseph and his coat of many colors, ya know that story?"

"Yeah, they hated him, right?" Austin said.

"Well, yeah, but what did Joseph do when he was confronted by his brothers after he was the governor of Egypt?"

"Oh yeah, he had that dream of them bowing down to him, and they did, that musta been better than revenge, right?"

"Yes, yes, then what did he do?" Uzziah prompted Austin.

"I don't know. I feel like I'm in Sunday School class, what did he do?"

"He forgave his brothers, and wept on their shoulders," Uzziah said.

"Yeah, like that's gonna happen," Immanuel said. He was raised up on one elbow and looking at Uzziah when he said that.

"How much did ya hear?" Uzziah asked.

"Enough to make me wanna puke, why?"

"Mr. Jones," Austin said.

"Who the hell are ya callin' Mr. Jones, call me Immanuel or don't call me nothin', ya hear?"

"Yes, sir—"

"And cut the sir crap, kid."

"Uzziah was telling me these things about us because he believes that it might mitigate your case with the authorities."

"How so, scribbler, how so?"

"Well, a man who had been wronged so grievously by his own brothers, and then instead of seeking retribution, simply gathered them back into the fold of his family, that man would be seen as something more than barbaric."

"Can ya translate Uzziah? It's a bit early in the morning for me to stand afore the jury and give a closing argument."

"Austin believes that if he writes about this reunion—"

"It ain't no flippin' reunion—"

"Ifn he shows ya to be a forgivin' man, then it's more likely that the government and especially the city of St. Louis, will turn around and offer the same forgiveness."

Immanuel looked between the scribbler, Austin Fielder, and Uzziah, his partner of many years. He knew what they were saying, but the idea of going into the camp of the Mandans up north and west of the fort, and doing anything but taking scalps, riled him something fierce.

"Immanuel, it's like theater," Austin said.

"Now ya done lost me fer sure, what's like theater?"

"What yer about to do."

"Ya mean I'd be actin' the part and not really meanin' it, then yer abso-fuckin-lutely right!"

"When the actors, for example," Austin began, "in one of Shakespeare's plays begins reading his lines when he is chosen for a part, do you think he believes everything he's saying?"

"He'd better or the damned audience will boo him off the boards!" Immanuel said.

"Exactly, so, for my article about what happened to the undersheriff in St. Louis, it would be better if there were mitigating circumstances—"

"That son of a bitch gutted that beautiful lady, and

that, my dear boy, is certainly a mitigatin' circumstance!"

"Exactly, and neither you nor Uzziah"—who had finished cooking their breakfasts and was now passing them out—"would have done such a horrific thing to an innocent man, right?"

"Right ya are, scribbler," Immanuel said and took an enormous bite of beans and bacon and chomped a biscuit in half and looked like a cow chewing its cud.

Austin ate a little bit, then continued with his argument, but not before he complimented Uzziah, "Um, good biscuits. Now, Immanuel, you have to understand that the people were dealing with they are faint souls. They are not in the habit of forgiving men for skinning an undersheriff who worked for the city of St. Louis, but if I investigate and find other examples of his cruelty and get those witnesses to talk to me so I can put their stories with yours, then they might begin to understand. You and Uzziah weren't the only ones who were done wrong by the undersheriff, but you were the only ones who took the law into your own hands because there was essentially no law or justice in St. Louis for you to turn to."

"Ya sure ya ain't a lawyer?" Uzziah asked.

"Been to plenty of trials, that's where they send the junior journalist, to cover trials."

"He's right!" Immanuel said, pointing at the young man with the other half of his biscuit. "Yer a good law-talkin' dog, ya are!"

"But here's the other side of that coin I just described to ya. You ready?"

"Sure, counselor scribbler, fire away," Immanuel

said, finishing off the first biscuit and sopping up with the other one.

"If I can include within the story of what happened to the undersheriff and give credible facts that support this was not the first time he had done such things, then I can lay it on thick about what you're really like, huh? A man who was wronged by his brothers. Uzziah told me the tale. A man wronged by his own flesh and blood—"

"I's only their half brother," Immanuel said.

"I will not stress that, but here, ladies and gentlemen of the jury is a man who went back to the place where he was betrayed, absolutely betrayed. They left the young boy for dead, but now, he returns to give them, and him, the satisfaction of a reunion in which no blood is shed, but rather, the Christian emotion of forgiveness abounds! What do ya say?"

"Ya know, jest 'cause I talk like this, don't mean I'm stupid. I done read Socrates, well, in translation a course, and he said, *To thine own self be true*, scribbler."

"Yeah, but when your emotions are involved, when passion takes the place of reason, are you really being true to yerself?"

Immanuel thought about that.

"Haven't ya felt like killing your own partner from time to time?"

"Well, I, that is—"

"But ya didn't, did ya? No, that would not have been true to your innermost self. In the same way, killing yer brothers—"

"Half brothers!"

"Killing your half brothers might feel good while it was happening, after all, they were cowardly and left a young man—they left you to die with the Sioux, but how would you face your ma then, how would you feel about that?"

"Maybe ya shoulda been a preacher, scribbler, maybe that would have fit ya better," Immanuel said, then added, "Anybody gonna want the rest of the beans and bacon, and how 'bout that last biscuit?"

The other two shook their heads that they did not, and Immanuel finished off breakfast.

———

They set out for Mandan Fort and along the way, Immanuel kept an eye peeled for random bands of renegade Injuns, and Uzziah and the scribbler, Austin Fields, worked on the script which they were going to teach Immanuel to use when it came to his—half brothers!

Uzziah kept seeing Immanuel looking at him, and he knew what he was thinking. He was going to let them make up whatever they felt like making up, but when it came time for him to face those bastards, he was just going to uncork it and let happen what happened.

But there was a slight, Uzziah admitted it, slight chance, since the scribbler wanted this bit of drama for the article which he was going to get published, and the scribbler assured Immanuel, without this piece of the puzzle, the rest of the story, the skinning of the undersheriff, for example, would be a hard sell for civilized folks. And yet, Uzziah believed that even if the article changed no one's mind, the performance of forgiving his brothers would change something even more important—Immanuel's heart.

They didn't make the time that they usually made because Austin Fielder was scribbling in his notebook in shorthand, as he called it, and looking over at it, Uzziah didn't know how in the name of God anybody could tell what it said. But Austin assured him when they rehearsed at the campsite that night, he would tell Immanuel everything his part entailed.

"Rehearsed?" Uzziah said, looking at Austin.

"Yeah, how's he going to make them believe he means it, if he doesn't practice?"

"He's right," Immanuel spoke up, and both Austin and Uzziah were surprised that Immanuel was paying attention.

"Ifn I lie poorly the lie will not lie well with those who receive it."

Uzziah was seeing a different part of Immanuel, a part that he was sure was going to disappoint both him and Austin when the actor, Immanuel, took to the boards. There was a lot of blood in Shakespeare's plays, and if nothing else, this *play* of theirs might just end up with death visiting all around and plenty of blood, oh yes, plenty of that.

They had eaten supper, and it was basically a repeat of what they'd had for breakfast, although Immanuel managed to bring down a small deer, and Austin vomited when Immanuel was cleaning it for supper. The boy tried to hide what he was doing, but they, both mountain men, saw.

"Now, ifn this was a paly, I wouldn't be believin' ya as a mountain man, I'd be knowin' that ya was a tender-foot. Didn't yer pa take ya huntin'?"

"No, my ma was a vegetarian?"

"Yer ma were a vegetable?" Immanuel asked, then

chuckled. "Nah I know what that is, people that only eat vegetables. Were yer pa one, too?"

"No, my pa and I ate meat, but we didn't hunt, my ma thought it was too cruel," Austin said.

"So, who cooked the meat in the house?" Uzziah asked.

"My pa and me, when I was older."

They ate, and Austin's appetite did not suffer from the freshly killed meat. In fact, he commented on how good it tasted, and Uzziah hoped he wasn't going to ask for a recipe.

The tin plates were being washed by Uzziah down by the stream when Austin got out the script he'd created and started talking to Immanuel.

"So, when ya first meet yer brothers, sorry, half brothers, will you recognize them?"

"I'll never forget them bastards!" Immanuel lied, trying even now to bring one of their faces to recall.

"Okay, so, the first meeting will be, and I'm leaving it up to you and Uzziah to arrange this, it will be in the teepee of your ma—"

"Ain't got teepees, they got mud huts, big mud huts, high ceilings," Immanuel said, remembering.

"Good, good, it will be more like a theater, then. Whatever order your half brothers are sitting in, I want you to change the order to the order of their births, with the oldest sitting next to your ma, okay?"

"I'm gonna tell 'em where to sit, why?"

"It's not important, just do it. Oh yeah," Austin said as Uzziah came back from the stream with the clean tin plates and put on more coffee, "they won't recognize you, will they?"

"They think I'm dead, young son, hell no, they won't recognize me."

"How 'bout yer ma, will she know who ya are?"

"Doubtful. Hell, she may be dead, don't know."

"Okay, we'll cross that bridge when we come to it."

"Isn't the White man always giving gifts to the Injuns?" Austin asked.

"Sometimes, why?" Immanuel asked reluctantly.

"Well, you won lots of money on the paddle wheeler, didn't ya?"

"Yeah, so?" Immanuel could almost tell what was coming.

"I imagine there's all sorts of trinkets and supplies at the Mandan Fort that your brothers and ma would like—"

"Ain't no fort, the Mandan burned it to the ground right after the expedition left for the West Coast," Immanuel said.

"I don't think it will work without the gifts," Austin said.

"Why! Just tell me why I gotta give 'em gifts afore I make an apology for what they done to me, oh hell no!"

"Okay, maybe we can skip the gifts—"

"Yeah, good idea," Immanuel said, then he went into a voice. "Hey, I am so sorry ya deserted my ass to the Sioux, and oh, by the way, here are some gifts fer doin' that! Ya get my drift, scribbler?"

They went back to practicing the lines that Austin had written, and when Immanuel wasn't laughing or cursing, it went all right. Uzziah kept looking at Immanuel and imagining that he could actually pull it off, it didn't seem impossible in lots of ways. The man had a temper on him, and Uzziah was sure that he had rehearsed what he'd really like to do to his half brothers long before they started in on this rehearsing.

Still, if the scribbler was going to write a piece about them, which he said he was, then it would be important for this part of the story to be told, a forgiving Immanuel who brought gifts to the family that had essentially betrayed him.

———

The next day, the day before they reached Mandan Fort, they camped in a real nice spot, beside the Missouri. Uzziah went fishing, and Immanuel had other plans.

"Don't wanna fish?" Uzziah asked Immanuel who usually liked the sport as something calming.

"Nah, got me plans to help the scribbler out," Immanuel said.

Immanuel walked over to where the scribbler was sitting up against his saddle and, par usual, scribbling.

"Hey, ya want me to gift my ma and half brothers, ain't that right?"

"Yes, that would be great for the story."

"Well, the fort was burned to the ground, like I said, under suspicious circumstances, afore old Lewis and Clark made it back after getting to the West Coast. My guess is the Mandans done it, but that's just my guess. But I do know somethin' that every Injun wants and needs and we're gonna get it," Immanuel said, and as he started walking away from the camp, Austin jumped up and Immanuel added, "Bring yer Springfield, will ya, and plenty of powder and shot."

Austin was so unused to being out in the prairie

like they were that he imagined the two of them, the mountain man and himself, might encounter enemy Injuns and have to defend themselves. They walked a good two, three miles from the camp and the shores of the Missouri, then Immanuel stopped and crouched down.

Austin Fielder was looking for enemies and was worried that they hadn't brought their horses, then Immanuel got on all fours and crawled forward to the top of the ridge.

Immanuel grabbed Austin's hat and took it off the boy, then the two men looked over the ridge. Down below them, near a pond, there were two good-sized mule deer—a doe and a buck, and two fawns.

Austin went back from their looking point on the ridge and turned on his back holding his Springfield.

Immanuel came down and whispered in his ear, "Young son, ifn ya want me to do somethin' that is basically agin my nature, you have to humor me and do somethin' agin yers."

"I can't shoot them, I can't!" Austin whispered to Immanuel.

"Fine, now ya know how I feel 'bout apologizing to the bastard half brothers and giving them gifts on top of it, but here's the thing, these deer dressed down and salted and taken to the Mandan village where my ma and her bastard sons live, well, trinkets are nothin' compared to somethin' that gives life, and these two deer would take that family well onto the fall. Now, what do ya say, help me kill these deer, and I'll get 'em all salted and cured and give 'em to the bastard half brothers who betrayed me, otherwise, yer story's gonna be lacking the proper ending, ya got me?"

"I don't think, that is, I have never..." Austin's voice trailed off.

"Is that thing loaded?" Immanuel whispered, "Better load it scribbler or yer story'll fall flat as a pancake."

Immanuel watched as, with shaking hands, Austin Fielder, the journalist who didn't mind eating venison, was going to get a firsthand experience on what it was like to kill one.

"Ifn ya miss, I'll know yer a yellow-bellied, no good, scribbler who just wants what he wants without payin' his way, ya understand?!? I done seen ya shoot, and yer a crack shot, ifn ya don't bring one of 'em down, this whole deal is off. I'll take the buck, he's liable to spook first, and it might have to be a shot on the run. Ya take the doe, the one with no horns, ya ready?" Immanuel asked as Austin had finished loading.

The boy had never killed anything. Well, that was a lie, he had killed a bird once with a slingshot, and he felt so bad about it, he gave the bird a proper funeral in his backyard and didn't dare tell his ma anything about it. And now, his Springfield was loaded, why did he bring the damned thing anyway—well, because he knew where he was going and he knew what he was looking for, and by golly he had found the real deal, the real McCoy and if he didn't kill a deer right now, then the story of a lifetime was going to go by the wayside.

He'd once asked his father if he'd ever killed a deer, and he had answered that he had, but that he could barely look at it afterward. The way its big, brown eyes still looked at him after it was dead made him feel awful.

Okay he wasn't a mountain man, but Immanuel

was right, if he really wanted this, if he was asking Immanuel, a real mountain man, to act as though he forgave his brothers, and if he wanted the story, then it was time for him to step up and do something in the mind of the man he wanted to write the story about to earn that right to do so.

"Ya ready, scribbler?" Immanuel asked, and both of them got on their stomachs and crawled to the top of the ridge where the family—well, that's what it was, a family of deer, a mama, a papa, and two babies who were enjoying the afternoon sun and a drink of cool water.

"Sight up now," Immanuel whispered.

They both sighted up, and Immanuel was right, the buck looked up and started moving as they both shot.

Immanuel was glad to see that the scribbler had taken him seriously. The doe ran a short distance then fell dead. The buck was only wounded, and he ran along with his two fawns away from the shooting.

"Load again," Immanuel demanded. They both loaded, and Immanuel was up before Austin. He sighted in on the tail end of the mule buck and fired. It went down, then he grabbed the Springfield and sighted in on one of the does.

"NO!" Austin shouted. "Not the babies!"

But Immanuel's shot with the Springfield was deadly, and the doe flipped end over end, and the other one came back to see what had happened.

Immanuel loaded his Hawken again as Austin began to walk away.

"Ya stay right chere, I needs yer help." Immanuel flipped over and sighted in on the fawn who had taken off after smelling his sibling. Immanuel laid very quiet, and Austin thought for sure that he was reconsidering shooting the second baby deer, but when the Hawken exploded and the second fawn ran a bit, then laid down, Austin came face-to-face with his deepest fears of the wild, wild west. It was brutal, savage, and as Tennyson had said, *red in tooth and claw*.

Immanuel and Austin walked down to the pond, and it was, to all intents and purposes, for Austin Fielder, the sight of a double murder. They knelt beside the adult deer.

"Just do as I do, and try to keep from throwin' up," Immanuel said.

He took his Bowie and Austin took the large knife which he carried on his belt, and which he'd probably never used till this very moment.

"Now, we're gonna make a cut around the butt hole of the deer," Immanuel said.

"What!?"

"I think ya heard me, son, now it's important if these *gifts* are not to be tainted, that you cut without severing the butt sack," Immanuel said and cut his ring around the anus of the deer. "Now, what the hell, son, start cuttin' or lose yer story!"

Austin did as Immanuel told him, and at this point, he was sorry he'd ever run into these two mountain men.

"Now, the same thing again, but this time go deeper, cuttin' all the ligaments that might be attached to the butt bucket," Immanuel said, and he did it and looked over to where, with a disgusted face, Austin was doing the same.

"Good, good work, son," Immanuel said. "Now, we're gonna lay these two big'uns with their heads uphill and their butts downhill." He turned his buck and Austin turned the doe.

"Now, I'm gonna hold the doe's legs open, and yer gonna put yer knife in shallow and cut an inch slit, right above the doe's milk sack, now do it!" Immanuel ordered, and Austin did it.

"Now, come and hold the buck's legs open fer me," Immanuel ordered, and Austin obeyed. By this time, he had grown numb to what they were doing.

Immanuel made the shallow slit, and then swift as a darting bird, he cut the buck's testicles off.

"What the hell ya do that for!?!" Austin asked, his face unmasked horror.

"Son," Immanuel said, holding up the bleeding nut sack, "these are a treat ya won't believe."

Austin thought about putting the bucks nuts in his mouth and almost lost it!

"Now, we're gonna take our knives and put our finger down with it to keep from cutting the guts, and we're gonna cut from the small cut all the way to the rib cage," Immanuel said and did so. The boy copied his cut on the doe. "Good, good work, ya may be a natural at this, Austin," Immanuel said, and the mentioning of his name made the boy think of his mother, and he almost broke into tears. He swore he would never tell her about this incident, ever!

"Now, son, we're gonna get on this cheer deer like we're mounting it to fuck it," Immanuel said, and he straddled the buck, and inserting the knife, facing toward the head of the deer, he cut through the ribcage and stopped at the neck.

"Now, well, yer just flowerin' me, that's good, don't

ever place the knife toward ya, or ifn ya slip, it'll all be over!" Immanuel warned.

The rest of the gutting went as Immanuel wanted it to, but when they pulled the organs out, and Immanuel took a bite out of the heart of the buck, Austin just looked at Immanuel's face, which was covered in blood from the mouth down.

"Here, ya take a bite," he said, holding the heart of the doe out for Austin.

"No!" the scribbler said, and Immanuel left it at that, or at least that's what Austin thought, but as he turned away, Immanuel jumped him, pinning his arms down with his legs, and he pushed the doe's heart in Austin's face.

"Take a bite, damn you!" Austin had the heart already in his mouth, so he managed a small nibble, and then Immanuel pulled it off his face, laughing the whole time.

"You're crazy!" Austin said.

"How do ya think I kept from goin' insane?" Immanuel said, then added, "I'll go get the horses."

"I'll come with you," Austin said, tired of seeing the slaughtered deer already.

"No, yer gonna stay and keep critters away from the meat."

"Critters, I don't see no critters," Austin said, his face just as bloody as Immanuel's.

"Well, load yer Springfield 'cause they's gonna be around, real soon," Immanuel said, then he took off in a shamble toward the camp.

When he was gone, he heard a shot, and then he jumped Trevor, grabbed the lead of Austin's horse, and took off. As he was leaving the camp, Uzziah came up carrying about a half a dozen fish—a catfish, a walleye, and some smallmouth bass. Dinner was gonna be a toss-up. That's the way it was in this life, either feast or famine.

"Is everything all right?" Uzziah asked.

"Dandy, never been better, partner," Immanuel said and rode off.

When he got to the dead deer, Austin was standing, loading his rifle again.

"What came our way?"

"Don't know, it looked like a mangy dog."

"Where is it?"

"Down there by the babies."

They gathered up the deer, putting a big one and a little one on each horse.

"There was a dead coyote down there, shot right through the head. Good shot, scribbler." They had to control Austin's horse, which had never, evidently, smelled that much blood. There was a pile of vomit where Immanuel had left the scribbler, and Immanuel figured the boy had earned his story. He knew he had to play his part—literally, but lying to women came naturally, so he figured it wasn't going to be that much of a stretch to lie to some bastard half brothers.

When they got back to the camp and unloaded the meat, Uzziah hung the deer up and started skinning them. Austin gave him a dark look, which Uzziah wasn't sure what it meant, then went down to the Missouri and washed his face for a longish time.

"What happened?" Uzziah asked his partner.

"The boy and I did a trade, he got to be someone he ain't and killed a deer, so's I can be someone I ain't and lie to my Injun kin," Immanuel said, and no more was said about it between the two mountain men.

Uzziah knew that there was going to be a price to pay by the scribbler, if, in fact, Immanuel was going to do the play they'd written. He thought that of all the things that could have happened, this one was the lesser of many evils. He wasn't sure the scribbler felt the same, but just so he was willing to write the story, Uzziah didn't really care. Immanuel got his pound of flesh, and it was probably only fair, probably!

———

They ate the fried fish in cornmeal that Uzziah carried in his deep saddlebags, and he made johnnycakes and, of course, beans and bacon. It was really a good meal, but Austin turned in early, and it worried Uzziah a bit. Maybe the boy would be gone in the morning? Who knew?

"Were ya rough on the scribbler?" Uzziah asked.

"No more so than he's gonna be on me," Immanuel said, picking his teeth with a fish bone.

Uzziah chuckled. "He sure got his initiation, didn't he?"

Immanuel started chuckling with his partner. "Yeah, in bloody spades! But we gotta salt and wrap the deer meat so it don't spoil."

———

In the morning, Uzziah got Austin to help him take down the carcasses of the deer and cut the meat into four-inch strips, then they salted it and added a bit of brown sugar that Uzziah had. He didn't have enough brown sugar, so he used the last of their white sugar, so it wouldn't be as sweet. They wrapped it in their deerskin clothes, which they took off, and threw all the meat on a travois behind Trevor. The two mountain men had only their breechcloths on, and every time Austin looked over at the big men in their whatever they were called, he just shook his head. These two men might as well have been from Mars, they were so different than anyone or anything he'd ever hoped to know.

6

They reached the Mandan village, the big one, where the burned-down fort used to be, and were greeted well by those who knew them, especially when Immanuel paid the man whose raft he'd stolen the last time they were through. Injuns think differently about things, and taking something that don't belong to you and basically getting away with the pelts you were supposed to pay them for the raft, well, they just waited to see if you could come up with some explanation and other payment. Which is exactly what Immanuel would do. The thing with Injuns was driving a good bargain for yourself and leaving the other guy wanting, so in that respect, Immanuel was looked upon as a good trader.

"I am the man you traded the pelts of your catching for the large raft, then you steal pelts back and take raft."

"Well," Immanuel said, trying to think as fast as he could, "it was the kid, Sahale, who told us where ya hid the pelts."

"My son, Sahale, has been dealt with. It is you who now must be dealt with," the Mandan warrior said.

"We have much deer meat, salted and cured for you and your tribe," Uzziah said, pointing to the travois that was covered by the deerskin clothes of the two mountain men.

Several riders rode to the travois and inspected the meat.

"However, not all of it is yours, father of Sahale. Half is, but the other half belongs to my mother, Shako-ka," Immanuel said.

"My name is Mato," he said.

"So, as a bear, you will appreciate that I did not take yer cub, Sahale, with me to St. Louis," Immanuel offered.

Mato looked at the other braves and they spoke quickly in Mandan, "But you also owe us for many canoes."

"If I remember, it was only two that were destroyed," Uzziah said to Mato.

"But many Mandan abandoned canoe that go down river and were lost," Mato said. His English was good.

"Have ya got enemies?" Immanuel asked.

"Yes, the Crow nation bothers us and raids our villages and steals our crops," Mato said. "In fact, most of those who used to live to the northwest have come here to receive protection from the Crow warriors."

"I can help you with the Crow," Immanuel said in Crow, and recognizing the language, many Mandans spoke it, they shrank back and raised their weapons.

"Can you become a war chief of the Mandans and lead us into battle against the Crow?" Mato asked.

"Yes and no," Immanuel said, this time in Mandan.

"You speak our language?" Mato asked.

"A little," he said in Mandan, then he added, "My first name was Pale Horse and my mother is Shakoka, who lived to the north and west," he said in Mandan.

Of course, Austin and Uzziah didn't know what was being said, but when some of the other warriors got off their horses and bowed down to Immanuel, they knew something was up. About half the warriors stayed on their horses, did not bow down, and glared at Immanuel.

"What the hell!?!" Uzziah asked Immanuel, "What kinda horseshite are ya layin' on these poor bastards?"

"You cannot be Pale Horse. He died at the age of twelve defending his family and keeping the north and west tribe of the Mandan safe. To his honor, we have a feast each year," Mato said.

"Well, be that as it may," Immanuel said in Mandan and it was coming back to him as he spoke it, "I am Pale Horse, and I have come to give my mother, Shakoka, and my brothers this gift from me."

The Mandan on the ground, who had bowed to Immanuel, now got involved in a long argument with the other Mandan, and Immanuel was having trouble following it. There were those who believed Immanuel was Pale Horse, and those who flatly refused.

"You will take the hut that you are given, and we will prepare to see if you speak the truth. To lie about such a thing is unforgivable, and if you are lying, you and your party shall be put to death!"

"What'd he say, Immanuel?" Uzziah asked.

"He says there's a hut for us to stay in, and it looks like we will be able to meet my mother and brothers soon."

"Well, there ya are, everythin's all set for yer performance, ain't it?" Uzziah said, smiling as he looked at Austin Fielder, who wasn't sure what he'd gotten himself into.

They were taken to the hut, and unloaded their supplies into it, and their horses were taken by the Mandan boys who took care of the horses and led them down to the Missouri, where they were herded with the other horses. Then, something unexpected happened, the warriors took the weapons of the White men, even their knives.

"What's that all about?" Uzziah asked.

"They're just being cautious," Immanuel lied.

"This is great, ain't it, partner. Ya can see yer ma and yer brothers and the scribbler can write the article we need about how ya found forgiveness on the plains."

"*Forgiveness on the Plains*, that's a good title for the story, Uzziah," Austin said.

"Thanks," Uzziah said.

Immanuel signaled to Uzziah that he needed to talk to him outside. Immanuel left the large mud hut, and there were Mandan guards standing around trying not to look like guards, but Immanuel knew.

"What's up, partner?"

"This thing with my ma, it just took an absolute jump in importance," Immanuel said, looking around at the guards.

"Whatcha talkin' 'bout?" Uzziah asked.

"It seems when I told them my Mandan name, they all went kinda berserk."

"Was that when some of them got off their horses and bowed down? What was that all about?"

"Originally, I was called Pale Horse. My father was

one of the men from the Lewis and Clark expedition. They believe that when I was abandoned to the Sioux, I was killed and was a sacrifice for my ma and brothers. That sacrifice saved the Mandans of the north and west."

"So, let me get this straight, instead of ya just tryin' to convince yer ma and saying ya forgive her and yer brothers for their abandoning ya, now, ya got to convince the whole village that you are who ya say ya are?"

"Yeah, that's about the gist of it," Immanuel said, looking at the guards.

"But there's more, huh?"

"A bit more."

"Just spit it out, Immanuel."

"Ifn they don't believe me, they will kill all three of us for desecrating the name of Pale Horse."

"What!? Yer joking, right, this is all to git back at me fer makin' ya come up chere and tell them ya forgive them?"

"No joke, ifn this was a poker game, the stakes have just been raised to life or death."

———

The Mandans, especially Mato, were smart. The legend of Pale Horse had been one of the most famous and widely celebrated legends of the Mandan's recent history. A half-White man had sacrificed himself so that his family could live. Perhaps it was the fact that he was half White that led the Mandans to put such faith in the legend. But each year, when the sacrifice of Pale Horse was celebrated, the brothers and the mother of

Pale Horse would gather with the tribe and tell stories of Pale Horse—his bravery, his cunning, his willingness to sacrifice himself not only for his family but for the entire Mandan Nation.

It was important for Mato to present the idea of this White man claiming to be Pale Horse in just the correct manner to the mother of Pale Horse. So, when he went to the mud hut of the respected Shakoka, he decided to, as the White man says, hedge his bets. He would tell her that before the yearly Pale Horse celebration, there was a simple matter that had to be dealt with, and leave it at that.

Mato didn't know which of the five brothers of Pale Horse would be there, and he sincerely hoped that none of them would be. Their mother had named them after the five original tribes of Mandan, which was seen as unusual even for those days. They were from eldest to youngest, Nup'tadi, Is'tope, Ma'nana'r, Nu'itadi, and Awigaxa. They were better known for their nicknames, Nup, Is, Ma, Nu, and Awi.

No one in the Mandan culture simply entered a hut that was not their own. They would usually stand outside the opening of the hut, and make noises, cough, or sing, but they never simply entered.

Mato sang a song he loved about the bears, and when Shakoka heard the song, she knew at once who was there.

"Come in, Mato," she said in Mandan.

"It is an honor to be in the hut of Shakoka," Mato said, waiting to be asked to have a seat by the central fire.

"Please join me at my fire," Shakoka said.

"It is an honor to join you at your fire, old wise one,"

Mato said, and then, after they were through with formal talk, they could get on with whatever conversation Mato had come to talk about.

She sat and was doing some beading work, and when she looked up, she expected him to get to the point.

"I have come on a delicate matter," Mato said.

She stopped her beading and looked at him. "Is it about the coming Pale Horse celebration?"

"Yes, in a way, but it's all very unclear in what way," Mato said.

"Please let me know."

"There are three White men who wish to speak to you and your surviving sons before the ceremony," Mato said, not sure what her reaction would be.

"Why?" she asked simply and went back to her beadwork.

"When three streams flow into one mighty river like the Missouri, it is impossible to say just which of the smaller streams should be spoken of first," Mato said.

She knew what he was doing. She knew the White men were the three streams—the Gallatin, the Madison & the Jefferson—and she knew that understanding all three streams at once would be impossible. So, Mato wanted her to float, stop, listen, and learn from each stream and then make her mind up. This was a way with the Mandan, and she appreciated the poetic use of his language, and not burdening her with things which would be better learned when she floated with each stream. Mato wanted her to wait and follow each stream from the big river to its source.

"Mato, you speak like the brother of a medicine man, which you are. I appreciate your fluency in the language of our ancestors and the lyrical way you put things. Sometimes, I think your father chose the wrong son to follow the medicine wheel," she said and stood up, which signified it was the end of the visit.

———

Meanwhile, back at the hut that the three White men inhabited and were basically prisoners, Uzziah had just finished explaining to Austin Fielder, also known as the scribbler, how much the importance of Immanuel's performance meant to the three of them.

"What?!?" Austin asked in astonishment.

"Ya didn't understand the man, or are ya askin' fer clarification?" Immanuel asked.

"The latter," the scribbler said.

"Look, it seems I've been a bit of a hit fer years and just didn't know it," Immanuel said and almost blushed.

"The Pale Horse celebration?"

"Right," Uzziah said, and then added, "Do ya remember in the Bible when Jesus went into his own hometown?"

"Bethlehem?"

"No, Nazareth," Uzziah said.

"That's right, he was just born in Bethlehem, then moved to Nazareth."

"So, do ya 'member when he taught in the synagogue at Nazareth what happened?"

"Not really," the scribbler said.

"Well," Uzziah said, "let me refresh yer memory." He pulled the Bible out of his saddlebags and turned to Mark, the sixth chapter, and then started reading.

"*He left that place and came to his hometown, and*

his disciples followed him. On the sabbath, he began to teach in the synagogue, and many who heard him were astonished. They said, listen to this. 'Where did this man get all this? What is the wisdom that had been given to him? What deeds of power are being done by his hands! Is not this the carpenter, the son of Mary, and brother of James and Joses, and Judas and Simon, and are not his sisters here with us?' And they took offense at him. Then Jesus said to them, 'Prophets are not without honor except in their hometown, and among their own kin, and in their own house.' And he could do deeds of power there, except that he laid hands on a few sick people and he cured them. And he was amazed at their unbelief."

And when Uzziah stopped reading, all three men looked at each other, and each was having thoughts of just how the Mandan people would kill them.

"We're basically screwed, aren't we?" Austin Fielder asked the two mountain men.

"Maybe," Uzziah said.

"And, maybe not," Immanuel added, then said, "In a poker game, it's fairly easy to take the game with a great deal of nonchalance, until that first hundred dollars is raised, then it's a game of another kind. No man can ignore the stakes after that first big raise. So, now that the hundred-dollar raise has been made—"

"They're going to kill us if they think you are lying!" the scribbler yelled.

"No need to start yellin'," Immanuel said. "After all, when the stakes get this high, then ya hafta take extra precautions."

"And what precautions would those be, Immanuel, since they've taken our horses down by the river, taken our weapons from us, and we are basically prisoners in this chere hut?" Uzziah asked.

"That's somethin' fer me to cogitate on, that's a fer sure," Immanuel said.

"Oh, my God, we are screwed, really screwed!" the scribbler said.

"There is the not-so-small matter of the Crows they got to deal with, and ya know I got an *in* with them, right?"

"Ya might have ridden Standing Bear's reputation a bit hard, don't know what it'll be worth in something like this with the Mandans," Uzziah said.

"Well, just don't count us out yet. We been in tougher situations than this," Immanuel offered.

"Name one?" Uzziah asked, and Austin Fielder looked between the two partners and put his head in his hands.

7

That night, after Fielder was sawing logs, Uzziah and Immanuel still lay awake in their bedrolls. The fire had died down to embers, but Uzziah heard Immanuel toss a log or two on the fire and move over to where he was sitting by the renewed flames. Uzziah got up, didn't say a thing, but poured fresh water into the coffee pot and then coffee into the percolator top, closed the hinged top, and placed it on the fire.

"I been thinking, partner, and I can't recall a single one of their faces," Immanuel said.

"Whose faces?"

"Whose do ya think?"

"But ya remember their names, right?"

"Yeah, sure."

"So, say their names out loud, wait a beat, and see what ya see," Uzziah coached him.

Immanuel looked at his partner of the mountains like maybe that wasn't such a bad idea.

"Okay, I will," Immanuel said, then he started.

"Nup'tadi, I called him, Nup," Immanuel said, and he closed his eyes and thought about his eldest brother. He could see Nup teaching him how to string a bow and how to bend the bow even when he was young, but all he could really see was the bow he had as a youth and the string for the bow that Nup handed him. Every time he turned to see the face of Nup, it was blurred, essentially a blank.

"I see what he taught me, but his face is not there," Immanuel said in a discouraged voice.

"Try the next brother," Uzziah encouraged him.

"The second oldest, wait, I almost saw his face, nah, it's gone. His name was Is'tope, I called him, Is. Huh, he was one of my favorites, I remember now. He taught me to swim in the Missouri, threw me in a swirlin' pool up against the bank. I think I swallowed half the Missouri that day," Immanuel said, chuckling.

"Close yer eyes," Uzziah said. "Try to see his face, just relax into it."

Immanuel sat there thinking about the day Is had thrown him into the river. He could feel the heat on his back, and the sun was beating down mercilessly, and he could feel the cold water that shocked his body and made him gasp for breath, then the struggle of paddling like a dog to get back to the shore, and Is crying out a war whoop when Pale Horse made it to the bank. Funny, that was the first time he had thought of himself as Pale Horse in forever.

"Well?" Uzziah asked.

"Nothin', brother, nothin'," Immanuel said, then he added, "But I am gettin' some sensual memories from those days. The next brother was Ma'nana'r—called him, of all things, Ma, but it don't mean the same thing as it means in English. I can't remember—wait, wait, he was there with Is the day I got thrown in. He jumped in and showed me somethin' besides the dogpaddle. He showed me how to swim, then held me in the water, and I swam, practiced swimmin' with him holding my belly afloat."

"Ya see his face?" Uzziah asked.

"Nah, nothin'."

"Who's the next brother, the fourth brother?"

"This is a waste of time," Immanuel said.

"No, no, it isn't, yer rememberin' all sorts of things and this will open pathways in yer mind to see it all, we can only hope," Uzziah said.

"Okay, the fourth brother was Nu'itadi," Immanuel said and laughed out loud. "He got me to race horses," Immanuel said. "What a horseman, oh my God, the man could ride!"

"You like horses, yer good with 'em, think what did he look like?"

"Nu was so gentle, the horses came to him, they couldn't resist his calm nature, they couldn't," Immanuel said, laughing out loud again. "I 'member this one time, there was this stallion, kinda like Shadow, except he was a roan, and no one could touch that horse, but Nu sat there in the field with him, and slept that night in the field, and when he awakened, who should be standin' over him to protect him? None other than that roan, and Nu just awakened, got up on him, and rode away. The horse never ever bucked, but no one else could ride him. What a man he was, that Nu!"

"His face?"

"Yes, I see him as clearly as I do you, Uzziah, I see

my brother Nu," Immanuel said, and tears were streaking down his cheeks, and he seemed not to notice.

Uzziah thought it best to go on. "Good, so ya saw yer fourth brother, maybe the rest will fit in. How 'bout the one closest to yer age?"

"Awigaxa, yes, but still, he was almost ten years my senior then. He taught me how to swear in Mandan, ha, ha." Immanuel laughed again. "Our mother, Shakoka, was so upset with him that she swore at him." Immanuel chuckled again. "And Awi said, 'This is where I learn all my bad words,' and Shakoka chased him from the hut, and all the way down to the river, swearing the whole way!" Immanuel's smile was broad and handsome, and Uzziah felt sure that doing this was all his partner needed to grasp the past in his mind and help him remember everything.

"You okay?" Uzziah asked.

Immanuel looked from the past, where his mother had chased his next older brother down to the Missouri, and into the present, where a man he dearly loved, and was his constant companion, sat worried.

"Don't worry, everythin' will be fine for Pale Horse, and those he cares for," Immanuel said as the coffee percolated, and he removed it from the fire. "This way we'll only have to reheat it in the mornin'. Thanks, partner, thanks." He moved to his bedroll, and so did Uzziah.

But Austin Fielder had been awake the whole time, and his doubts about not being killed the next day had only grown. He did not know Immanuel the way Uzziah did, and he had not witnessed the awakening in Immanuel's mind to his past. So, when he could hear the two mountain men snoring, he gathered his things, such as they were, and crept from the mud hut.

The guards were sitting by a fire not far away, but they were having a good conversation and did not notice the youngest of the White men escape toward the river, where he hoped to find his horse. He had brought his saddle and bridle, and even the sound of the tack gently tinkling did not alert the guards as he made his way to the river.

———

There was a great deal of shouting in Mandan, and those who were shouting were at the entrance to the White men's hut, and also standing in the hut. Both Uzziah and Immanuel sat up, and it didn't take them long to see Austin's saddle missing, and they knew what had happened.

Fairly soon, Mato came into the hut.

"Your friend has escaped, and the others think since you speak Crow that you are Crow spies, and that he has gone to warn them or even bring them here to destroy us," Mato said in Mandan.

"I am a friend of the Crow, but this youngster has only ridden with us less than a week. His honor and ours has been besmirched with his cowardice."

"What will you do to make it right. You who call yourself Pale Horse." Mato asked sincerely, Immanuel could tell.

"Let my partner, Uzziah, take his horse, Shadow, and run after the boy."

"Can he track?"

"Well enough. How far could he have gone? His

horse is much less than Shadow, and if Uzziah is not back by noon, then tie me to the stake and light a fire beneath my bones," Pale Horse said. He was proud of how well his Mandan was coming back to him.

Mato said something in Mandan and pointed at Uzziah.He had no idea what was going on.

"Go, they will bring Shadow up here, you must find Austin and bring him back before the sun is in the center of the sky," Immanuel said, mixing his Mandan metaphors with his English.

"Or what?"

Immanuel drew his thumb across his throat, and Uzziah immediately had fire lit beneath him, and he was up, carrying his saddle, and there was Shadow at the hut entrance.

Uzziah mounted up, and Immanuel extended his hand, and the two men shook arms like the Injuns do.

"With prejudice?" Uzziah asked.

Immanuel shook his head up and down. That meant whatever it took, even if he should have to wound the boy, bring him back.

Uzziah put his spurs to the belly of Shadow and the horse was out of there in seconds, clearing the village with Uzziah's head to one side as he followed the only shoed prints there.

———

Two hours had passed, and when Uzziah came upon the dead horse, he was not surprised. It was flecked with soapy sweat, and its tongue lolled out of its mouth. The boy, Austin Fielder, had run his mount into the ground, an unforgivable thing in the west. No man worth anything did that, no man who knew horses, or respected their lives, that's for sure. And this was the same boy who had objected to killing deer that were food. Sometimes, the objections of the civilized made no sense in the greater picture,

Something passed by his head like an angry bee, then he heard the boom of the Springfield. Uzziah did something which he thought Immanuel would be proud of, he grabbed at his chest and slipped from the horse and onto the ground. From the range Austin had fired, he was too far away to see properly, especially with those three times opera glasses. Uzziah figured all the boy wanted was his horse, but he was surprised he was willing to kill for it.

He lay there, and Shadow stayed right there as if Uzziah were playing some game. He hoped the horse would at least allow him to mount up, then it would be all over for the boy. He must have been quite a distance, because when Austin showed up, he was breathing hard.

"Good boy, good boy," he said as he walked past what he assumed was the dead body of Uzziah and grabbed at the reins. Of course, Shadow ran away a bit, stupid boy grabbing at anything around a horse was liable to get any horse spooked. Uzziah surely hoped the boy would get real and come at Shadow a bit more calmly.

"Sorry, boy, sorry, I shot your master, but I can't stay and be burned at the stake, it's against my religion," he said, and Uzziah almost chuckled, but remembered his partner back at the Mandan camp, ready to sacrifice his life if they didn't make it back in time.

Finally, Austin Fielder, the scribbler as Immanuel

called him, managed to get Shadow's reins in his hands, and the horse shied away and Austin had to circle with the horse to maintain control, sort of, then Shadow stood still. Looking under his bent arm, Uzziah could see Shadow's eyes on him when Austin got into the saddle and clicked the horse up the way he had heard Uzziah do.

That's when the rodeo started and Uzziah sat up, and out of the corner of his eye, Austin, the murderer, saw his victim sit up and smile.

Shadow didn't need to do too much with such a greenhorn, and the second time he shot into the air and bucked when he came down, Austin landed on his back, and when his head snapped back, he was out like someone had blown hard on a candle.

Uzziah got up and checked the boy's pulse, he was still alive, and frankly, Uzziah didn't give a shite one way or the other. He tied the boy to the back of his saddle and lit out like a shuck on fire.

———

It was still an hour before the sun reached its meridian, and Immanuel was standing with Mato outside the mud hut which the three White men had shared. When Uzziah pulled up, Immanuel breathed a sigh of relief, and Mato spoke up.

"This young man should be punished."

"We will wait until I have met with my family and the matter of who I really am is discovered before any more threats are made, Mato!" Immanuel said, walking right up to the Mandan brave and standing in his space. Mato backed away, and for just a split second,

Uzziah could see that he, Mato, was beginning to believe that Immanuel was Pale Horse. If it could be proven, then, of course, everything changed—absolutely everything.

"We will see when you enter the hut of the one who gave birth to Pale Horse, and then and only then, will you speak to me as you have," Mato said.

"Then, what are we waitin' fer? I'm ready right now, let's git this show on the road!" Immanuel said, and Mato wasn't sure what Immanuel meant.

"Let's visit the mother of Pale Horse and find out who is lying and who isn't," Uzziah said in broken Mandan—if he stayed here much longer, he might actually pick this language up.

"But first," Immanuel said in Mandan, "you will send someone to help the young man who tried to run away, and you will do it now!"

Mato scoffed and snorted his displeasure at being ordered around by a White man who was a pretender to the legend of Pale Horse. Mato said something to some Mandan Squaws standing nearby, and they immediately went into the hut to tend to Austin Fielder.

"Pale Horse thanks you," Immanuel said, and again, there was a snort from Mato, and he led the way to Shakoka's hut. There didn't seem to be anybody around, but that mystery was solved when they pulled back the deerskin opening to the hut.

When Uzziah followed Immanuel into the hut, it seemed as if the entire village had squeezed into the old woman's hut. There was an older woman seated by the fire. Most times, the person whose hut had been entered would be seated there, but Immanuel took one look at the old woman and had no recollection of her at all.

"What's the matter, Pale Horse? Why don't you greet your mother?" Mato asked Immanuel.

It was a darn trick that's what it was. Immanuel looked at Uzziah, and both men knew this trick, they could have seen it coming a mile away. If Immanuel went and greeted the older woman as Shakoka, they would be led to their deaths real fast.

"Where is my mother?" Immanuel asked Mato in Mandan.

"Are you blind? She is seated at the fire, there," Mato said, pointing to the imposter. Boy oh boy, Immanuel wanted to slap the bejesus out of Mato for leading him into this trap, but instead, he started looking around the hut. There must have been close to eighty people in there, and with all the body heat and the little fire in the middle, everyone was sweating. Every face that he looked at looked back at him, except for one older woman who seemed to be preoccupied with the hem of one of her sleeves.

Immanuel made his way through the crowded hut and stopped in front of her. When she looked up, he was transported back fifty years to the ravine where they lay waiting to die, and then he could hear the shouts of the Sioux taunting them to come out and die like braves. The look on his mother's face that day was tormented. She was going to die with her six sons, and her heart was breaking.

"Shakoka, look at me," Immanuel whispered in Mandan, as she looked up, her face changed just a bit, but he knew somewhere deep within her, she had the first inklings that this might be her Pale Horse.

"You are a dirty White man, and nothing more," Shakoka said, but her words rang false.

"Do this dirty White man a favor and come sit by your fire," Immanuel said, and taking her hand, he raised it to his lips and kissed it, something he had done as a child, something which had always brought a smile to his mother's face, and for a flash the smile started but was extinguished by a greater fear. Could she have not known all these years that her Pale Horse still wandered the prairie like a scorned ghost?

Immanuel led the woman whom he called Shakoka to the fire, and as they approached, the other older woman left the fire and joined the teeming crowd in the hut.

Shakoka sat by the fire, and Mato wondered if, when he had visited her when the White man had first arrived, had Immanuel had the opportunity to see this woman, and know whom Mato had gone to talk to—or, was this a man or a conjurer?

"Now, will my brothers step forward?" Immanuel asked, "Now that I have proven I know who our mother is."

Mato made a sign with his hand and all the men stood stock still.

Again, Immanuel looked over the crowd of men. He knew about how old they would be, and he hoped that since he had seen Nu'itadi's face last night when Uzziah was making him think about his brothers, and yes, there he was standing right up front looking older, wiser, but not trying to hide from his little brother.

Immanuel knew that when he picked Nu'itadi from the crowded hut, he must keep his peripheral vision looking for signs from the other men. He had already picked out those who were of the right age, so he would watch them when he took Nu'itadi in his arms and spoke into his ear, he might recognize another.

Immanuel walked directly toward the man he knew was his fourth brother from the eldest, and taking the Mandan brave in his arms, Nu'itadi did not resist the arms of Immanuel/Pale Horse as they encircled him, and he spoke into his left ear, "Nu, how are the ponies?" Pale Horse asked.

Nu pulled back from the hug and smiled. "They are plentiful as the grasses of the prairie," Nu said, and they hugged again.

Nu joined his mother by the fire, and they whispered back and forth as Immanuel had seen one man in particular swear an oath under his breath when he hugged Nu. That must have been Awigaxa, the brother who swore like a sailor, if they had known what sailors were.

Pale Horse pointed at his youngest brother and swore an oath in Mandan at him!

Awi broke into tears and made his way to Pale Horse, and they, too, hugged. Awi swore some more, and their mother, Shakoka, swore at him, telling him not to swear, and everyone in the hut laughed.

Is'tope gave off a war cry as he had done the day he had tossed Pale Horse into the mighty river, and those around him shrank away. It was becoming obvious that this was Pale Horse. He came from the crowd, and he, too, hugged his brother.

"He taught me how to swim, and gave that same war cry when he threw me in the Missouri," Pale Horse said, his eyes misting now. Then he looked around and saw another man moving toward the center of the hut, it was Ma'nana'r, who had gotten into the river with Pale

Horse and taught him something besides the dog paddle. They hugged, and Pale Horse had but one brother left, the eldest. He saw him now, and Nup'tadi and Pale Horse pretended to take arrows from their quivers and notch them in their bows, and pulling back on their imaginary bows, they let their arrows fly, straight to each other's hearts.

Then, if all that weren't proof enough, Pale Horse arranged his brothers from the eldest to the youngest, with the eldest sitting next to his mother, Shakoka.

"On this day, many years ago." Pale Horse was about to expose them—all of them—his mother and his five brothers, for deserting him to the Sioux, when a memory hit him like a herd of buffalo!

They had not left him. He, Pale Horse, had insisted they leave him. He, Pale Horse, had willingly stayed behind so that his mother and his brothers could live another day. Why, why had he forgotten such an elemental fact? How could he have thought that these wonderful people would desert him, the youngest, and how had he convinced them to leave him? Then Nup'-tadi, his eldest brother, stood.

"We celebrate the Pale Horse of many years ago, who bravely allowed his family to escape the Sioux's wrath. But we never discuss what Pale Horse, the 12-year-old warrior, said to his family to make them leave, do we?" he asked and looked at his mother and five brothers, who looked down at the ground.

"He insulted all of us, called us savages, saying that he would rather be with real warriors, the Sioux, and be raised as one of them rather than to stay with a bunch of farmers, do you remember, Pale Horse?"

Immanuel remembered all right, it was the hardest

thing he'd ever done in his twelve years on this earth to denigrate his mother, Shakoka, to say those horrible things to his brothers that he loved—well, like brothers, but he also remembered that if he had not spoken as he had spoken, they all would have died, and he would not stand for that.

The hut, with nearly all the village packed inside it, was quiet for a moment, then Shakoka stood and spoke.

"My son, Pale Horse, was fathered by Patrick Gass, one of the men who came with Sacajawea and the whites under Lewis and Clarke. I was a widow, if any of you are old enough to remember, and Patrick built me a wonderful home there at the fort. I did not intend to have his baby or in any way to lie with him, but I was lonely, and so was he, and things happened. I am not apologizing for my son, Pale Horse, who saved my entire family, but maybe I am telling you this again, for those who have chosen to forget, so that you will understand, Pale Horse thinks like no Mandan who ever lived. He was born unafraid to die, and I cannot tell you how happy it makes me and my family to celebrate this Pale Horse celebration with the very man who made it all possible."

She finished and was about to sit back down when Pale Horse grabbed her and they hugged. She broke down into tears of joy, and as Immanuel/Pale Horse was also about to join her in weeping, a Mandan brave broke into the hut.

"A Crow war party is coming!" he shouted, and the hut emptied out like water from a broken jar.

Outside the hut, Uzziah grabbed Immanuel. "What's happening?"

"The Crow have decided to raid us," he said as he

whispered to a Mandan boy who rushed away toward the river.

"What are we gonna do?" Uzziah asked.

"How can I ever thank ya fer what ya have done fer me? How? If there was ever one man who was in debt to another, it is me, so indebted to ya, my brother, my friend," Immanuel said, and then he yelled into Uzziah's face. "Wagh!"

"Wagh!" Uzziah yelled back, and all the Mandan thought the two White men had lost their minds.

"What are we gonna do 'bout the Crow?" Uzziah asked.

"We're not doin' anythin'," he said and jumped on Trevor's back. The horse was bareback and had a war bridle on, and the boys had painted him. There were swirls and red handprints, and arches over his haunches.

"Wait," Uzziah said, "ya can't face a whole war party on yer own!"

"I'm not," Pale Horse said as his six brothers rode up on their painted ponies. Someone handed Immanuel his Hawken, it was loaded, and the others had rifles and bows and arrows.

As Immanuel and all his brothers rode toward the Crow war party, who had been in some way shamed by the boy, Pale Horse, who had saved their lives, those same men now rode proudly with the man, Pale Horse, who had made them all proud.

As they got closer together, Immanuel thought he recognized one of the figures riding with the braves, but dismissed it as wishful thinking, then both parties pulled up about thirty feet from one another, their horses prancing in the dust of the prairie. The fight would begin when the first warrior rode toward the other group.

There, sitting his horse, as proudly as any Crow brave, sat the medicine man's son, a bit older, but ready to take the fight to the Mandan village.

"How is your father, the medicine man?" Pale Horse spoke in Crow to the boy.

"He fares well, and our people have done well since the buffalo run and have also been gifted with the women who were stolen by the Comancheros. I heard you had something to do with that," the boy said, his horse prancing, ready to ride into the battle.

"It was the power of Standing Bear that rode with me as we took back the hostages of the bad hombres," Pale Horse said.

"So I heard. I should not be surprised that you ride with the Mandans, but certain things always surprise. We will leave the Missouri Mandans alone now and fight no more forever with them," the boy said, and turning their horses around, the party of twenty Crow warriors rode away.

"They are afraid and have ridden away. We will go after them and kill them all," Nup'tadi, his eldest brother, advised.

"Not today, Nup'tadi, not today," Pale Horse said as he circled Trevor painted up like a war horse and rode him slowly back to the village.

EPILOGUE

The celebration at the Mandan village was next to none according to all those who had celebrated all Pale Horse Day before that. What amazed Uzziah was how sober Immanuel managed to stay, and how he was even respectful of all the women that Uzziah knew wanted him to come to their mud huts.

"What's goin' on, partner? Ya don't seem yerself," Uzziah said as he sauntered up to the man that he had looked up to for all these years.

"I'm not myself, I'm somebody else, but I ain't sure who yet," Immanuel said.

"Well, I think ya might take a bit of Pale Horse back to the mountains with cha, couldn't do no harm."

"What are ya tryin' to say, young son, Pale Horse is a better man than Immanuel James Jones?"

"Speaking of that, where in heaven's name did ya come up with that name fer yerself?"

"I like Immanuel from the Good Book, James was

the brother of Jesus, and I once knew a man named Sam Jones, who had a beautiful wife, Mrs. Jones."

"Yer so full of shite," Uzziah said. "Makes me wanna go get the last bottle of bonded from the scribbler."

"He got one left?"

"Yep, though, he may not write that article now that we chased him down, and he's the most unpopular man in the Mandan village."

"I could give a shite, so go get the bottle, young son," Immanuel said, raising his eyebrows and tilting his head toward their mud hut, where Austin had basically stayed, recovering from his rodeoing experience.

"Okay, be right back," Uzziah said and wondered why he had brought up the bottle when Immanuel/Pale Horse was doing so well without it.

Inside the hut, Austin Fielder sat with his pad in his lap, and he was scribbling away to beat the band.

"Whatcha writin' scribbler?" Uzziah asked.

"Just the best story that was ever written about you guys. I am gonna get things straight and get the authorities to drop the charges on ya, and maybe, just maybe, we can get the US Marshal's office to investigate the sheriff's office of St. Louis," he said, his smile as big as Uzziah had ever seen him smile.

"You owe us," Uzziah reminded him, "and that reminds me, where's that last bottle of bonded?"

"I'm going to keep that," Austin said.

"Not after running yer horse into the ground, and takin' a shot at me, then tryin' to steal my horse, yer not! Now, let's try this again, where's the bonded?"

Fielder's smile disappeared as he went to his saddlebags and got the bottle. "Ya ain't ever gonna forget what I done, are ya?"

"Nope, and ifn yer gonna pout, just remember, I ain't told Immanuel that ya tried to kill me and take my horse, ifn I did, ya wouldn't be able to write the article."

"Why not?" Fielder protested.

"Dead men don't scribble," Uzziah said, and taking the bottle, left the hut.

————

Meanwhile, Immanuel saw a White man in one of those long, black robes—a Catholic priest, known among all the Injuns as Black Robes. It sure looked like he was coming Immanuel's way, so he started to walk off, and the priest called to him.

"Pale Horse!" he yelled. What the hell, secrets sure travel faster than just about anything in the world. Immanuel turned and faced the man.

"Whatcha want, priest?" He got right to the point, he was about to get into some bonded, and he sure didn't want this man's preoccupation with God's rules getting in the way.

"Congratulations are in store, I understand," the priest said. He was of medium build with a lot of black hair on his head and a beard that went well with the robe, and a huge crucifix hanging from his neck. He couldn't help but think of Coleridge's Rhyme of the Ancient Mariner and the line, *"Instead of the cross the Albatross about my neck was hung."*

"Whatcha talkin' 'bout?"

"I know your mother, Shakoka, and knew yer pa, too," the priest said, expecting Immanuel to ask him some questions, and when he just stood there looking at the priest, he continued, "Your father came back several times to look for you."

"And?"

"He cared about you, Pale Horse," the priest said, hoping that that would open Immanuel's heart.

"Yeah, he built my ma a house and knocked her up, that shows a lot of caring."

"She burned the house down, she was so ashamed," the priest said.

"Sure, she did," Immanuel said, being sarcastic.

"When the Lewis and Clark party got back here, they were rather surprised that the Fort had been burned down. She didn't intend for that to happen, she had only wanted to get rid of the house he'd built her and left her with child."

"Yeah, funny how things can get out of control like that," Immanuel said and stared at the priest.

"Wouldn't you like to know about your father?"

"Nope, I sure wouldn't," Immanuel said and saw Uzziah walking up with the bottle. "So, my partner's returned, and as far as I'm concerned, this talk is over, priest," Immanuel said and walked toward Uzziah.

The priest looked at the two mountain men. He had dealt with men like that before, or so he imagined that both of the men were basically the same—he couldn't have been more wrong, but that's the problem with stereotypes, they aid a person till they don't.

———

They saw Austin Fielder off at the dock where he boarded a paddle wheeler for St. Louis. He had wanted to assure both mountain men that he had enjoyed their company and would surely write the article he had promised about forgiveness on the prairie, but no sooner had they made the docks than the scribbler turned around, and the two mountain men were riding off without so much as a goodbye.

Well, he knew he deserved that. He had come into the plains and the west with no code appropriate for such a place, and in the middle of everything, had lost his nerve and almost committed murder. He had had every intention of killing Uzziah and taking his horse, and no amount of thinking about that scenario would change what he had done, or was willing to do.

He had a suspicion that Uzziah had finally told Immanuel about it, and that was the main reason for the cold leaving. He assured himself that he was lucky that the older partner hadn't killed him after finding out about his betrayal, and it seemed to him that the far west and the Rockies were a place where betrayal and double crossing were something more common than not. Still, he did not like to think of himself as the sort of man that he obviously had proven himself to be. He vowed to write the article and have it published, and who knew, maybe that would repay his debt to Uzziah and his partner?

———

Both partners headed straight for the mountains and their cabin homes. They talked little about the scribbler, and Uzziah figured since he had told Immanuel about what the boy had done, that that was probably for the best. He saw in Immanuel's eyes a hard glint when he told about being shot at by the boy, and all Immanuel did was reach across and hold his partner's arm for a moment, give it a squeeze, and they rode on.

Sometimes, friends have so much water under the bridge that anything said, things about what had happened, wasn't as important as riding on, going over the next ridge, the next hill, the next mountain, and getting on with being the free men they imagined themselves to be.

MOUNTAIN MEN
MURDER TRIAL

1

It had been a while since Uzziah and Immanuel were able to stay in the mountains and do what mountain men do. They trapped for the fall pelts, which are never as plush as the spring ones, and they were able to gather enough wood, and shoot and jerk enough meat that the winter, which was strangely mild, was not oppressive to them.

Immanuel read from the collected works of Shakespeare and they decided to take different parts in *The Tragedy of Hamlet*. They read the play sitting right next to each other, sharing the book. Immanuel teased Uzziah mercilessly that his Ophelia was better than the one he'd seen once back east, perhaps Uzziah had missed his true occupation, playing women's parts in Shakespearean plays?

The reading continued, but Uzziah hadn't taken the comment of him playing lady's roles lightly, and before Hamlet met his untimely death, Uzziah and Immanuel managed to destroy the cabin where they were reading the play and beat each other almost to a pulp. They finally had to stop the fight because in their rousting about a lantern had been broken and the coal oil caught fire, threatening to destroy all the cabins.

They fought the blaze even though both of them were bleeding from the fight, and when the fire was finally extinguished, the cabin with the potbellied stove —Uzziah's cabin—had been nearly burned to the ground.

"Ya see what ya done!" Uzziah said to Immanuel.

"What I done?"

"Yeah, never say somethin' like that to me, ya hear!" Uzziah said.

"Ya mean 'bout ya missin' yer proper career of playin' lady's roles in the theater, is that what yer talkin' 'bout?"

Uzziah glowered at Immanuel. "Ya burned down my cabin," he yelled.

"Ya gonna cry 'bout it like a girl?" Immanuel asked, and the fight was back on.

They rolled around in the hot ashes, taking punches at each other, and yelled from time to time as either one or both of them rolled into hot embers. Finally, they got up and decided they'd better put out all the embers before they caught the rest of the cabins or even the forest on fire.

"I ain't forgot what ya said," Uzziah said, now nursing swollen burns on his shoulders and back.

"Well, that's just great, 'cause I ain't forgot how well ya read them girlie parts." Immanuel came back and they were bowed up again when one of the hot spots flared up and they had to fetch water from the stream to put it out.

Uzziah moved what was left of his possessions into

another cabin, but grouched well into the night at his partner for starting the whole ruckus. Immanuel got drunk and passed out before Uzziah could land his emotional and well-thought-out barbs concerning his partner's argumentative nature.

Immanuel was passed out before the fire, and Uzziah was feeling the difference in the temperatures of the two cabins. The one he was supposed to move into had not been heated at all that winter.

"To hell with it, I'm movin' in chere," Uzziah said to himself since Immanuel was snoring.

Uzziah brought his bedroll and some of his cooking things into Immanuel's cabin and built a fire in the one he'd eventually move to, so it could warm up.

————

Uzziah rested well that night and got up early since he hadn't been the one drinking all that much.

He built up Immanuel's fire, got water going for grits, and made the biscuits to throw in the Dutch oven. They had gathered some mourning dove eggs, well, he had, while Immanuel walked along beside him, trying to figure out a way to apologize for his comments that night and the fire that had destroyed the cabin with the potbellied stove.

"I ain't never been good at saying I'm sorry," Immanuel began.

"Should be easy since yer the sorriest person I ever met," Uzziah said.

Immanuel had plenty to say to that, but because he couldn't remember exactly everything he'd said that night, the whiskey was doing that to him nowadays, he just kept his mouth shut.

Uzziah was glad Immanuel was making the effort to go with him to gather quail eggs, the effort said a lot in and of itself. They, the two of them, had become so used to being around each other that they had learned a sort of shorthand of actions. Sometimes, just making an effort was enough.

They got back to the cabins, and his old cabin was still smoldering. They went on into Immanuel's cabin and Uzziah got them ready to scramble. The bacon was sizzling nicely and the biscuits were just about ready when Immanuel's appetite woke up.

"Ya plannin' on stayin' in chere?" he asked friendly-like.

"My new cabin is warmin' up, I'll sleep in there tonight," Uzziah said as he continued with the breakfast.

"Ya slept in chere, last night?" Immanuel said, seeing Uzziah's bedroll.

"Yes, I did."

"After all that insultin' I done ya?"

"Yeah, it's hard to be mad at a drunk," Uzziah said, slipping the Dutch oven from the coals.

Immanuel thought about that for a moment and let it go. Uzziah was right, it was hard to be mad at a drunk, and being called one wasn't that insulting, he did like his liquor.

A truce was reached and they kept stoking fires in the cabin which Uzziah was supposed to inhabit, and two or three days later, he moved in, much to Immanuel's delight. Though, if he admitted it, he liked them sleeping in the same room. At least he had someone to annoy.

———

By later in the spring, the fight had been forgotten, and rebuilding the cabin with the potbellied stove was on the agenda, but first, there was the spring laying out of traps and such. Even though beaver was bringing poor rewards, it seemed the two mountain men, and invariably good friends, could not stop doing what mountain men had always done.

They scheduled the rebuilding of the potbellied cabin, they were now calling it for summer, when they could work without worrying about keeping warm. They fished and hunted, then played cards. Sometimes they played poker, even though Uzziah knew that Immanuel was cheating, and then they got out a cribbage board which Immanuel had found in the ruins of the potbellied cabin. Uzziah then became the champion of that game, being in better possession of numbers than Immanuel, and as yet, Immanuel had found no way to cheat in a six-card game, where two cards were given back to the dealer and then the game played.

Uzziah kept winning, but was sure that, at some point, Immanuel would find a way to cheat, and he would know as soon as Immanuel started winning. Immanuel whined that he wanted to play poker, but whenever he did, he cheated and invariably won, which took them back to cribbage, where Uzziah was champ.

———

Back east, in Baltimore, Maryland, exactly, well, not right in the city of Baltimore, but in the outlying areas, Patrick Gass sat on his stoop and surveyed his farm. He had over two hundred acres and horses, milk cows, and plenty of timber. He had married Harriet Somme, the daughter of a French merchant in Baltimore, who still imported various luxury items from France. Monsieur Somme had dreamed that his daughter would marry a bit higher than she had, but Patrick had notoriety as one of the members of the Lewis and Clark Expedition, and his journal of that expedition was the first published of all the journals.

Patrick and Harriet had raised five children, three boys and two girls, all of whom were grown, and three of them moved away, well, not that far away—the one boy had become a lawyer in Baltimore, and the two daughters had married influential men, and they both live with their husbands in Washington DC.

Harriet had tried to teach Patrick French, but he hadn't had the desire to learn, and now his French was like that of a five-year-old. Still, they loved each other deeply, and his exploits before they had married were not only well-known, but published.

She had read in his published journals how he had fathered a son among the Mandan Indians and built them a house before he continued on his way west with the expedition. She accepted this, as any good French woman would, for was not France the country where most successful men were married and had mistresses? At least what had happened with the Mandan woman had happened when he was a bachelor, and even though he had made trips to find his son, and been totally unsuccessful, she knew that Patrick was faithful to her and her alone, and that she treasured in her heart.

Patrick was staring at the road into his farm, and thinking that perhaps he would try macadam, which was the invention of a Scotsman John McAdam, back in the 17th century. The one thing that Harriet hated was the tracking in of mud, and in spring and fall, the road out there from the main road was nothing but mud. Macadam would fix that and make him even dearer to his lovely wife.

Patrick was contemplating how pleased Harriet would be when the mailman drove down the muddy road and Patrick went out to greet him.

Patrick walked to the carriage that delivered the mail, and he and Burt, the mailman, started ribbing each other the way they did every time Burt had an opportunity to see the *Gasman*, that's what Burt called him.

"When ya goin' to get a real job, Burt?" Patrick teased.

"Well, at least I work, I can see ya out here half the time just sittin' and ponderin' yer fate," Burt said, and the two men chuckled.

"Well, as I might've told ya, my family goes all the way back to the Battle of Hastings—"

"Oh, my Lord, are ya gonna bore with that history lesson again, Gasman, really?"

"Anything interesting?" Patrick asked, knowing that Burt looked at all the mail he delivered.

"There is one from way out west. The sender's name is Father Albert Margaux, sounds like a Frenchie, maybe Harriet's old boyfriend?" Bart teased.

"Well, if he had known her, he certainly wouldn't

have turned to the priesthood," Patrick said, always looking for an opportunity to compliment his wife.

"Well, I'll be dying to know 'bout that one," Bart said as he clicked up his horse, made a U-turn in the muddy road, and waved as he trotted his horse back out to the main road.

Patrick walked back into the house, and the smell of cinnamon rolls filled his nostrils as he walked toward the kitchen.

His wife, Harriet, walked out, drying her hands on her apron. "Anything for me?"

"Yes, there's one from your sister in France, and a couple of catalogs," he said as he took his letter and sat down in his favorite chair in the parlor. Harriet watched him go and wondered who had written him, but was so interested in the news from France that she took her letter and walked back into the kitchen.

Patrick got his reading glasses from the inside of his vest pocket and, placing the ear grabs behind each ear, he took his pocket knife from the right pocket of his trousers and sliced open the letter.

Dear Mr. Gass:

I am Father Albert Margaux and I am a Catholic priest sent to bring the message of our Lord Jesus Christ to the heathen. I travel a great deal in my occupation, and many times by canoe. One of the tribes I visit are the Mandan people. I think you are acquainted with that particular tribe.

A few months back, I witnessed the return of a man to the northwest Mandans who had long been thought to be dead. This discovery by his mother, Shakoka, surprised the Mandans quite a lot.

I know that we met when you had first been back

from the Expedition with Captains Lewis and Clark, and I also know that this same Shakoka had been with child after the Expedition came back through. I realize your duties precluded your staying here to be with the Mandan woman and you returned to the east.

But I did meet you when you came back out and saw your infant son, who could not have been more than a year and a half old. I remember you tried to convince Shakoka to come back east with you, but the stories which the Mandans had brought back from Washington were not to her liking, and she decided—against your advice—to raise the boy with the Mandans.

Subsequently, the boy's disappearance when a group of Mandan hunters were overrun by the Sioux resulted in the assumption that the boy had been killed. He was not, evidently.

Before I left the Mandan village, I was approached by one, Austin Fielder, a journalist who said he was going to write an article about your son, Immanuel, and his partner, Uzziah. He told me that he owed it to these two mountain men because they could have done a lot of things to him, which they declined to do because of their forgiving natures.

He told me of a crime, I'm not sure what to make of it, but it seemed to have been committed in Saint Louis, and both, your son Immanuel and his partner Uzziah Ferguson O'Bannon, were implicated in the crime. That's all I know about it, but there was a hint that there was something grizzly about the events that surrounded the disappearance of an undersheriff in Saint Louis.

He swore to me that the article written by him will exonerate your son and his partner in the death of an undersheriff in Saint Louis. He was young, though, and anxious to leave the territory, so I'm not sure how much faith we can put in what he said, or in his ability to write such a story.

At any rate, I thought you should know that the son you sought before he was a grown man was not killed by the Sioux, and his presence here was totally accepted by his family, and I can't imagine a more thorough vetting process than that of his own family members.

I hope this missive finds you in the best of health, and pray that the Lord has blessed you with this news of a son, much like the prodigal, who was thought to be dead, but is now alive!

Your Most Humble Servant,

Friar Albert Pierre Margaux

Harriet wandered into the parlor with a fresh cinnamon bun on a plate. When she saw her husband's slack face, she put the plate down on the table next to his chair and seated herself on the ottoman in front of him.

"What's the matter, my dear? Is it bad news? Has someone died?" she asked those two questions while taking his hand into hers. He raised his other hand with the missive in it.

"Quite the contrary, my dear, if this letter is to be believed." His voice was rising with every word, and by the time he finished the sentence, he stood. "If this letter is to be believed, my son, you remember, the one I told you about from that Mandan woman? My son is alive!" He took her in his arms, and she screamed a joyous sound, and they hugged each other tightly.

She took the letter from his hand, and as he walked about the room, not quite sure what to do next, his hands to his head, she read the letter.

"This seems a most trustworthy source of information, Pat, it does!"

"Yes, yes, I know, but what to do next, what to do next?"

She sat him down. He was the dreamer in the family, true, he was a magnificent carpenter, father, and husband, but she was the one in the family who balanced their budget, told him what he could spend, and she had the level head. Then, like a good wife, she handed him the plate with the warm cinnamon bun on it. He began to eat as she talked.

"Patrick, listen to me. I think what you need to do next is to hire a detective, someone maybe in the police department, who could go to St. Louis, we have plenty of money for the future. Hire this man, and have him question people who were involved, see what the circumstances of the death of the"—she paused here as she looked back at the handwritten letter—"the undersheriff. Surely, a person of astute mental capacity could find out what we need to know about this so-called murder and set things straight. And, if it took more than that, then do we know a wonderful lawyer?"

"Monty," Patrick said, "Montague, our eldest son, he's a very good lawyer!"

"There you have it, we won't even have to pay him, he would be just as interested in this man, who, indeed, might just be his older brother, wouldn't he?"

"Of course he would, but I'm worried," Patrick said.

"About what?"

"About you, me having a son was all hypothetical, yes, I mentioned it in my journals, but all this was simply words on a page, and now, there is a real grown man out there, and it seems his mother is still alive."

"So?" she said, accenting her French accent just so. "What have I, Harriet Josephine Somme have to worry about some Mandan woman from forty years ago, huh? Now, if you had a mistress here in Baltimore, well, that would be an insult of a different color, and even though I am French, I would not stand for it!" she said, smiling all the while.

He took her in his arms. "You are an amazing woman, Harry," he said, he kidded her like that by calling her by a man's name. She wiped the excess frosting from his lips and put it in her mouth.

"Harry is the best woman you could ever have married," she said as they laughed together.

———

Baltimore, Maryland, was a harbor city, and the harbor itself docked ships from around the world. The city itself looked like a Grecian festival of white buildings, which seemed to rise out of the inner harbor to the top of the hills surrounding the city and where the Columbus Obelisk was built to commemorate the founding of America. It was prosperous, and it liked to think of itself as a modern city where the savagery of the past had been subdued and now cosmopolitan citizens wandered its vast streets, buying and selling the wares of the world.

The city had been established in 1729 and named after the Irish barony of Baltimore, which was the seat of the Calvert family, who were the proprietors of Maryland.

Maryland itself, had been established for Catholics —a place where those who were not Puritans could live in peace and not be hounded by Puritan law. It was literally the Land of Mary, the mother of Jesus. It became a port where grain and tobacco were shipped out of to Europe, and before the Revolutionary War, it was a shipbuilding center with Baltimore clippers making runs to the Caribbean, where they traded for rum and other items. When it was feared the British would attack Philadelphia, the Continental Congress met in Baltimore to continue their talks of succession from the British Empire.

It was into these environs that Patrick Gass made his way by carriage. He had hired a hack to take him to a specific address, and he was rather surprised at the neighborhood which he was now entering. It was not one of the most fashionable, and it was too near the docks to be considered anything but a place where a man might meet his demise, at least, at night. It was the middle of the day, and he'd found the address at the publishers.

The hack pulled up, then turned around.

"Sorry, Governor," the man said in a British accent. "Gone too far toward the harbor." Then he went back up Light Street to Baltimore Street, turned right, and north toward Amity Street. Finally, he pulled up, and the neighborhood was much better, and the little home which bore that address was modest, but rather nice.

He told the hack driver to wait, then walked up the four steps to the front door, and knocked on the tall white door with a four-paneled framed glass transom above it. There was no immediate answer. He looked above, and there were two shuttered windows on the second floor, and they were both open to let in the light, and a rather large shuttered window to his right, which was closed. The house was made of bricks.

Patrick could hear mincing footsteps coming to the door and he waited. The door opened, and a very attractive young lady of less than twenty years opened the door.

"If it's a delivery, can you come around the side door?" she asked.

"No, no, I'd like to speak to Mr. Poe."

"Are you from the publisher?"

"No, but that is where I got his address."

"I'm sorry, can you write my husband a letter about what this concerns, and he will reply, I assure you," she said about to close the door.

"Look, I am willing to pay and pay generously for Mr. Poe's advice," Patrick said, and miraculously, the door was reopened to its full extent.

"Please come in," she said, and when he stepped inside, he saw that the home was nicely arranged and quite tidy. The front room, the parlor, was lit by a lamp in the corner. There were red drapes pulled apart, which looked out on what seemed to be a sitting garden, very popular for city people who had no land. On the wall to the left was a pastoral painting of woodlands and water, and commanding the middle of the room, a marble table which was octagonal. Writing materials were on the desk, and a single chair was pulled up to it. Some papers had been written on, and they were in one stack, in the other stack was fresh, unused parchment.

"I will get Edgar, he's out back," she said, and walked to another part of the house, and Patrick went to the window. He could see a man sitting in a broadcloth coat with no hat, and he was simply staring into the garden. She, the young woman, approached him and touched him on the shoulder. He seemed neither shocked nor surprised that she was there. He looked up at her and smiled. There was a stark contrast in their ages, and when she spoke to him, his head turned toward the window. Patrick was looking out, and momentarily their eyes met. The man stood, and Patrick got away from the spying window.

When he entered, Patrick was surprised by the narrowness of his shoulders and the head, which seemed hard to maintain on such a foundation. His high forehead gave him the appearance of going bald, but he did, in fact, have a great mane of black hair attached to the cranial capacity of a large brain. The eyes were sad, and bags drooped from them, and there was a perpetual wrinkle between and above the sad eyes that pointed to a long nose, which ended at a mustache that was exactly the width of his slash of a mouth—absolutely no lips at all—snake mouth, was Patrick's first thought. The cravat about his neck was loosened, and only the top button of his vest was fastened, and his coat open.

"How may I help you?" Poe said in a voice both deep and resonant.

"I am sorry to barge in like this, but I would like to hire the services of C. Auguste Dupin," Patrick said, and he noticed that the young woman looked at Mr. Poe oddly.

"Could you make us some tea, dear?" he asked in the kindest of voices.

"Certainly," she said and left the room.

"Please sit," Poe said and gestured toward the divan. Patrick sat, and Poe sat at the table, not where he had sat to write, but in the chair closest to the door, and turned the chair toward the divan.

"So, you want to hire an imaginary detective, interesting. Why would you make such a ludicrous request?"

"My reasons are simple, my son and his partner have been accused of a murder in which there is no body, well, they can't find one, and the man killed was an undersheriff in St. Louis. Almost all the evidence, I believe, which points to these two men having done the crime is by circumstance only. They were in the city when the crime was committed. Soon, after the undersheriff disappeared, so did they. It seems to me to be for want of a real suspect, the sheriff and the good citizens of St. Louis have filled in the blank with men who are not of their ilk."

"You sound like you've already solved the murder," Poe said.

"Hardly, I—that is, my son and his partner—need a mind which can—like Auguste Dupin's—look passed the crime and into the circumstances surrounding it."

"And yet, Auguste Dupin is a fictional character in a short story I wrote and had published entitled, **The Murders in the Rue Morgue**, and nothing more."

"So, you don't think like Auguste Dupin at all, do you?" Patrick asked Poe.

"Well, I—"

"Where am I from?"

"What?"

"You already know where I come from, don't you?" Patrick asked him.

"The country, but you have manure on one boot heel."

"And why am I from the country, the streets full of horse manure?" Patrick asked.

"True, but you gazed out a window in my house, a window which you had to cross the room to look out. City people, when they come into a stranger's home, do not do such things."

"Why?"

"Because the city is more compact than the country, looking out a country window will afford one only the view of country-living—barns, horses, cows, and farm machinery. But looking out a window in the city could show you things which are personal, especially a window in the back wall of a house."

"I bow to your ratiocination, Monsieur Dupin," Patrick said, and he made a mock bow from the divan.

"Surely you don't think that the murder you're referring to was done by an orangutan?"

"No, but you must remember that my son is half Indian, half Mandan to be exact, and surely you have to admit that as uncivilized as an orangutan is, this murder may shake your faith in civilized man, who in the guise of a Mandan warrior, may, in fact, be more brutal than any other of the primates," Patrick admitted.

"While I appreciate the fact that you not only read the short story, and I imagine, enjoyed it, but I like to write every day, and traveling to St. Louis is out of the question," Poe said as he stood.

"Has your wife been to St. Louis?" Patrick asked as the young lady came in with the tea.

"She's young enough to be my daughter, why do you call her my wife?" Poe asked, and the young woman blushed.

"But she isn't, she's Virginia Eliza Clemm Poe, your

wife," Patrick said, then apologized, "I'm sorry, but this matter is much too delicate and too important for any mind but yours to be considering it," Patrick said. "I took the liberty of writing down exactly what I am willing to pay for your services," he said and handed the folded slip of paper to Poe.

Virginia grabbed her husband's dangling arm, leaned in closer to her husband, and watched as he opened the slip of paper. Their eyes grew wide at the figure scribbled there.

"Oh, Eddie, please, let's go. You know I've never been west of Columbus," Virginia said as she clutched at his arm.

Poe looked down at the amount on the paper, and letting go of his wife's hand, he stretched his hand out, and the two men shook.

"Yes! Yes!" his wife said as she kissed him on the cheek, and it was his turn to blush.

"I have done lesser things in the past for much less money, and I can only assume I will do lesser things in the future for much less money," Poe said, rationalizing his desire to both please his young wife and earn the amount for the job.

"Everything you need to know about the so-called crime, and the names of my son and his partner are in these notes," Patrick said as he handed Edgar an envelope.

"You seem rather assured that I would, in fact, take on this wild goose chase," Poe said, fingering the envelope, finding its thickness.

"You are first and foremost a man who loves mystery, and if this isn't a mysterious murder, I can't think of what else would be?" Patrick said as Poe walked him to the door.

"We shall leave, Ginny and I, on the next B & O train to St. Louis." The two men shook hands again as Patrick walked out to his hack.

As Poe closed the door to his house, he turned to his wife, Ginny, as he liked to call her.

"Darling, there will be a lot of time that I have to spend searching out answers in St. Louis, into places that I would not dare take you," he said, holding both her hands.

"You know I can amuse myself, don't I do the same thing here when you are entranced by the blank page that you feel compelled to fill?"

He kissed both her hands. "Yes, yes, of course, I am sorry. I leave you to your own devices too much, don't I?"

"Nonsense, your work is my work, darling," she said, kissing the hands that held hers.

2

It had been a while since the two mountain men had been to Vrain's. They lacked a lot. The coffee that they had was poorer since Uzziah had found chicory growing in the lowlands and had supplemented the coffee with it. It would have tasted fine if they weren't used to just plain coffee. There was also a simple lack of just about everything else they needed for Uzziah to do his cooking, and as any married man knew, once you grow accustomed to good cooking, it's hard to look the other way when it goes downhill. Not that Immanuel would have considered Uzziah his wife, but the general notion was there. Uzziah did the cooking, and Immanuel did most of the hunting. They had set their spring traps and had found plentiful beaver with great, long fur and plush beyond what they had seen in a long time.

"Ya know why this beaver's so good, don't ya?" Immanuel asked as they were stretching out the pelts on the circular willow branches.

"Why?" Uzziah asked, concentrating on what he was doing.

"'Cause nobody wants it anymore. Ifn we were in a seller's market, we wouldn't have found any pelts like this," Immanuel remarked.

"That's just plain stupid. The beavers don't know their pelts are worthless," Uzziah said, scoffing at the same time.

"Then tell me why these are so plush? It weren't even a hard winter, these pelts should be thin and gross, but they ain't, and the reason they ain't is 'cause we're bein' mocked by the beavers," Immanuel said.

"I cannot doubt that this is the way yer thinkin', but please, ifn ya don't mind, keep such mindless drivel to yerself. It ain't worth thinkin' 'bout."

"I know ya think beavers can't mock us, but how many times ya seen beaver prints around a trap and no beaver?"

"They're just smart, that's all," Uzziah said.

"Smart aleck is more like it, they know dern everythin' 'bout what we're doin' and they're throwin' it back in our faces!"

"So, they saw how plush their fur was and committed suey-side just to git at us?" Uzziah asked.

"Yep," Immanuel said as he began stretching another plush pelt.

Uzziah grinned and shook his head.

They finished the stretching, laid them out nice, got mounted up, and headed for Vrain's.

———

The trip down was pleasant, they saw lots of deer, which Immanuel pretended to shoot by holding out an imaginary Hawken and killing them.

"They mockin' ya, too, by being right around when ya ain't huntin'?" Uzziah asked.

"Now, yer talkin' like a real mountain man!"

When they got to the Vrain Trading Post, the men, both buying and selling, started up a ruckus.

"Well, well, ifn it ain't the most famous men this side of the divide," Jean Baptiste said, and everyone turned and started yipping and whooping it up like they were somebody besides themselves.

"What in tarnation had gotten into ya bunch of flea baits?" Immanuel asked.

"Only this," Jean Baptiste said in his heavy French accent as he held up an edition of the St. Louis Daily Evening Union. "It's the big article—the one with both yer names over the top."

Immanuel looked at the section entitled, *Only in Saint Louis*, and the headline read:

```
The Killing of Undersheriff Randall
              Hicken
       as told to this reporter by
Immanuel James Jones & Uzziah Ferguson
             O'Bannon
          By Austin Fielder
```

"What the hell?" Uzziah said, his mouth agape.

"I already read it," Jean Baptiste said, "and I did it out loud to these guys, how 'bout a bottle of our finest to share while ya read?"

"Sure," Immanuel said. "Should I read it to ya?" he asked Uzziah.

"Nah, I'll just hang back and read over yer shoulder," Uzziah said.

Immanuel sat down and read, with Uzziah right behind him. The article filled most of the page and the next. The print was fine, like most newspapers, and there was a lot of reading to be done. They had a couple shots each as they read, and Uzziah had to wait on Immanuel to turn the page, since he was, in fact, a faster reader.

When Immanuel was done, he sat back and looked at Uzziah, who shrugged.

"That son of a bitch set us up!" Immanuel said.

"Well, he certainly told it with the passion which we felt at the time, but I wasn't so sure he was going to just lay it out there. I mean, he even included the wood station, and what we done to the man," Uzziah complained.

"He weren't no man and he deserved ever' cut," Immanuel said. "That Austin Fielder really cooked our gooses."

"And where's the part 'bout yer return to the Mandans and the honor they gave Pale Horse when they discovered who ya were?" Uzziah asked.

"Not there, brother man, not there, but he made sure that they knew ya was there, too!"

"Yeah, like I needed to remind him," Uzziah complained.

"Well, ya fellas," began Jean Baptiste, "ifn I was either of ya, I wouldn't be showin' my face in St. Louis for the next hundred years."

"That's the only savin' grace," Immanuel started in. "Thank God he didn't have no drawin's of us."

"Feel like maybe we oughta get back at him somehow. Don't think he liked what he done to us at the Mandan village, runnin' like that, tryin' to shoot me off Shadow and all," Uzziah said.

"Yeah, ifn I'd have known all that afore he left, he wouldn't have left alive," Immanuel said.

"But I thought the article might do us justice," Uzziah said, pouring them both another drink.

"Fat chance," Immanuel said, picking up the shot and slamming it back.

They saved the rest of the bottle and decided to get back to the cabins and figure all this out, if there was any figuring to be done. They bought all the supplies they needed, trading a lot of their plush pelts for pennies, Jean Baptiste was whining about the silk market taking over from beaver, yeah, yeah, yeah, they knew!

The ride back home was through much of the same territory, they didn't like to make a trail when they went back and forth, so they altered their way to and from most places, just in case. And now, the just in case had to take into account the fact that a bounty would probably be laid on their heads, and if they weren't careful, the next time they went into Vrain, there might be an unfriendly gun or two waiting on them.

"Hell of a thing," Immanuel said, and Uzziah had nothing to say, since that sort of covered the whole mess, it was a *hell of a thing*. Uzziah also knew that sensational articles like that would be picked up by other papers all over the country. He hated the idea of his ma, Rahab, reading it, and all his brothers and sisters thinking their worst. Now, he knew that they were independent thinkers and all that, but still, public opinion can work havoc on a family, and Uzziah wondered how long it would be before merchants in the Shenandoah Valley would be cutting off his pa's credit, or demanding payment before anything was ordered and delivered?

Mostly, he hated the fact that the young minds of his brothers and sisters might be turned against him. He didn't worry about Sarah, she would think what she wanted to think till the day she died, but he just hoped she wouldn't get herself fired up or worse, standing up for him and Immanuel. But what could they do now, and especially this far from the problem? There wasn't anything. One thing was for sure, they had basically been condemned to the Rockies for the next ten years or so. They didn't mind that, but it was one thing to want to stay there because you were a free man, but quite another when you started thinking that the government would get involved if they showed their faces in St. Louis, much less Virginia.

———

The wind was blowing that particular morning in Chicago, Illinois. The wind, though, wasn't the problem. It was one of the huge great lakes, as they were called, Lake Michigan, most certainly that took that wind, filled it with moisture, and as anyone knows, when the cold hits you with cold and humidity, that's when it's really cold.

Kate Warne, a woman not young, but not old, hurried her way down Washington Street, lowering her head and thankful that she had a hat pin to secure her, well, not fashionable but practical hat, which was shaped like a man's bowler, but curled ever so lightly in the front. There was a hatband which surrounded the crown with a buckle on the right side, and from that buckle, identical stripes matching the hatband radiated from it—four to be exact. Regardless, she did place her hand on the top of the hat, it wasn't that expensive, but still, she wasn't made of money.

She looked up and saw that she was coming to the Pinkerton Agency address at 69 W. Washington Street. Lake Michigan was to the north of that particular building, and not that close, really, well, twelve blocks, but the wind made it feel as if the lake were directly beside the building. The building was neoclassical in form. It had columns out front and resembled the architecture of ancient Rome in a sense. She entered the building, said hello to the building superintendent who sat at a desk out in the lobby, and took the wide staircase which came down both sides of the second floor, turned right, and walked down to Allan Pinkerton's office.

"Good morning, Miss Warne," Pinkerton's secretary said. "Do you have an appointment?"

Kate ignored the woman and walked to Pinkerton's private office door.

"Mis Warne, oh, Miss Warne..."

The rest of what she said was muffled by the thick oak door. The door reopened, and the secretary was standing there with the door in her hand. "I asked her if she had an appointment!"

"She's welcome anytime, it's okay," Pinkerton said.

Kate stood at the edge of his desk, a veritable siege of energy emanating from her. She was holding the

Chicago Weekly Democrat in her hand, the paper was open to one particular section. "Have you seen it?!?" Warne didn't ask this, she demanded an answer.

"Take it easy, you're much too young to have a stroke, but the way your face looks, it worries me."

"My face is telling a story, and I think you know what that story is," Kate Warne said.

"Sit down, or better yet, have some tea or coffee, it's all on the sideboard over there," he said as he gestured with a cultured hand.

"I don't want tea, I don't want coffee, I want these two men!" she exclaimed, throwing the newspaper down. The same headline had been used, it seemed, by all the papers that picked up the story. Pinkerton looked down at it. He had already read the article that morning over breakfast, it made a most entertaining tale.

The Killing of Undersheriff Randall Hicken
as told to this reporter by
Immanuel James Jones & Uzziah Ferguson O'Bannon
By Austin Fielder

Pinkerton looked again, if nothing else, to satisfy this woman who had enough energy to run Chicago itself, if they could harness it.

"Do sit." This time, it was not a request, it was an order, and Kate knew it. She sat down and she harrumphed when she did so, and so did the cushion on the chair she threw herself into.

"What are we going to do about this!?!"

Allan looked at her and, picking up the paper, he

perused the article again. He had already decided what he was going to do, and if Kate Warne hadn't shown up in his office, which he was sure she would, he would have sent a messenger to her house and requested her presence. And yet, Kate usually knew what Allan was thinking, and he dismissed that as something men say when they really have no idea what women are thinking, but wish to think they did.

"Well?!?"

He looked at her over the top of the newspaper, and he smiled. She sort of smiled back.

"Do you have any idea how the sales of this newspaper skyrocketed this morning?"

It wasn't a question that she had come prepared to answer, in fact, it was the last thing on her mind when she read the article. But leave it to Allan to think in the biggest picture possible, and in this case, it would have included the sales going up with this sensational story within its pages. She hadn't answered, so he continued.

"Word of mouth still is the fastest form of communication, same as gossip, I imagine, but a bit more sophisticated. Someone read this first, then they told someone else, and that someone told five people, and that someone told ten—"

"Is there a point to all this!?" she demanded.

The point was to make her wait, and that was exactly what he was doing. She was his best detective, even if she was a woman. Hadn't she had the younger of this duo under arrest in cuffs, or tied up, he couldn't remember, but she had gone on a hunch, taking with her an inept new Agent, who it turned out, had trouble hitting the broadside of a barn with his weapon, but she had them, well, one of them. If the other, the older man, hadn't pulled off a trick almost as great as the French illusionist, Jean-Eugène Robert-Houdin, then she would have caught the other one.

Her embarrassment at being set adrift on a paddle boat whose paddle no longer worked and the fact that those two had laid out there and shot the mechanism that worked the paddle wheel to hell, well, that would have been enough. But later that same year, she got a tip that Uzziah was visiting his sickly mother in Virginia. She had taken the famous Indian tracker Abooksigun with her and 50 US Cavalry troops and had them in sight, not once, but twice, only to be foiled, and then the word had come they had won a horse race back in St. Louis, the scene of their original crime.

Well, it was too much for Kate Warne. She had taken a leave of absence, gone to the Riviera, that's what she called Cape May, and relaxed, but when she came back all tanned, all she could talk about were these two mountain men, simpletons, who kept outsmarting the elite of lawmen.

"Well, Allan, really, are you trying to drive me insane?"

"No, you are probably the person best qualified for that job. I have already taken steps—"

"What steps?"

He put his index finger to his lips, which was his way of telling her to shut up! She took the hint.

"I have contacted the Democrat and requested an address on this Mr. Austin Fielder—"

"What on God's green earth will that accomplish?!?"

He gave her a look and she settled back down.

"He got this story directly from them, but as you

and I both know, this is a *he-said-she-said* kind of story, and legally it cannot, will not, and should not stand up in court." He paused there to keep her from jumping out of her chair. If he had been a schoolteacher, she would be the girl in the back frantically waving her hand, sure that she knew the answer.

"But I want them for the murder of our Pinkerton Agent Robert Spells!" she veritably shouted.

"Yes, yes, and so do I, but first things first. Do you fish?"

She thought that an odd question, but was willing in an employee-employer sort of way to answer. "No, it's a disgusting pastime."

"Perhaps, but what every fishing expedition requires, my dear, is bait."

He could see that this line of reasoning was getting her where she lived, her mind was racing, and if he waited long enough, it would catch up with his, but he wanted the coop.

"We need bait, and this article about the killing of the undersheriff is good bait."

She said something she rarely admitted, but Allan Pinkerton did have his ways about him, and one of them was a mind that thought laterally.

"How is this article bait?" she asked, resigned that he was way ahead of her.

"What if there was a bounty put on their heads, a bounty that could not be ignored by those mercenaries in such a profession?"

"But who would do that?"

Allan lowered his head and looked at her from just under his brow.

"No!?!"

"Yes," he said, and then continued, "I decided that most of the bounties offered in the west are ridiculous and encourage men of low degree to go after the money. Most are under a hundred dollars, and you and I both know that Robert Spells was worth more than that."

Pinkerton knew that Kate had thought of Spells as a younger brother, and warned Allan not to send him after the two mountain men, but Pinkerton liked the boy's pluck and sent him anyway.

"So, how much would you imagine would bring about an all-out hunt on the two men?" she asked.

"A thousand dollars would do it, I imagine."

"But who would..." She stopped there and wondered, then Pinkerton continued.

"An anonymous benefactor, someone who tired of the west throwing their lawlessness and their lack of morality in the faces of good, upstanding citizens in the populated and cultured centers of the east, perhaps?"

"You would—"

"My name and the name of the Agency will never, ever be associated with the bounty prize, and if it is, I'll know where the information came from," he said, pulling out one of the cigars from his drawer that he smoked when a particular point had been made or an argument settled. It was a sign that everyone who worked for the man recognized, and even though Kate wished to discuss the ramifications of this bounty and the what-ifs, well, the discussion was over.

3

The day was pleasant and dry. That was one thing that both mountain men like about the weather in the mountains, mostly it wasn't damp. This splendid summer day was one that both men cherished. The clouds were puffs high and blowing over the peaks, there was no sign of rain, and certainly nothing to say about snow at all. Most of the higher peaks had lost their snow, with a few of the four-teeners still hanging on to the vestige of last winter's snowfall.

They had finished with the stretching of the pelts they had caught in the spring, and even though they were both disturbed by the article in the newspaper they saw at Vrain's, neither of the men gave it a second thought. Well, that wasn't exactly true. Immanuel had gone over—several times, it might be added—what he was going to do to the scribbler if ever they should cross paths again. But in reality, they knew the charges that had been lowered on them in St. Louis would probably be something that hung in the back of their minds for the rest of their lives.

It was only Uzziah who had hoped that all the charges would be dropped. If the scribbler had done what he said he was going to do and bring in the forgiveness side of both men, how Immanuel had been united again with his Mandan family, but there wasn't a drop of ink on that particular angle of the story. What Uzziah worried about was how much difference in age there was between himself and Immanuel. There was no denying that Immanuel was twenty years his senior. That difference did not show itself now, the man, Immanuel, as stout and fit as he had ever been, but there would come a time, perhaps a time when Immanuel would need the help of a doctor, well, Uzziah sort of doubted that, since the man had so many remedies of his own. But still, Uzziah was thinking about all this when a stick of dynamite, its fuse growing shorter by the second, dropped right in between the mountain men.

Immanuel, being the fool that he was born to be, picked the short-fused sputtering stick up and chucked it as far as he could. Unfortunately, it didn't have time to get there, but exploded about halfway to, and robbed a few ponderosas of their branches. Being immediately denuded, the air filled with the exaggerated smell of line, and the sound of the explosion nearly deafened both men.

"Run!" was all Immanuel said as he picked up his Hawken, which was his third arm, really, and Uzziah did the same, and they headed for the forest. Before they'd gotten fifty feet in, another stick of dynamite exploded behind them, and turning, Uzziah could see that the cabin that they had rebuilt, the one with the potbellied stove in it, the one which was originally his, the front of it was torn off by the explosion, and he could hear shouts of joy further away from where they were headed.

They got as far as a gully which was north and east of the cabins, and panting, they had run faster than two fat mountain men should have to run. They looked over the edge of the gully, which ran water in spring, and looked back where the dust was clearing from the second explosion.

"It's got to be Roscoe," Immanuel whispered.

"Who?" Uzziah couldn't wrap his mind around that.

"You know Benjamin and Roscoe," Immanuel whispered.

"They're our friends, and right and good fellows, why would they—" was all Uzziah got out before the cabin next to Immanuel's exploded, and timbers went flying high into the air.

"Ya know how we thought nothin' would come of that article the scribbler wrote?" Immanuel asked in a whisper.

"Yeah."

"Well, this is the fallout," Immanuel got out before another explosion ripped through Immanuel's cabin.

"Good thing we put the horses and Jenny on the highland pasture," Uzziah said, knowing that by now Jenny would have kicked down the barn door or been hurt in one of the explosions.

"Yeah, good thing, now let's get out there and get some distance from here," Immanuel said.

They hiked up to the high meadow, the place where

Leah's pa was buried, and as they went, they kept hearing explosions.

"Them sons-a-bitches are gonna destroy everythin' I built!" Immanuel said. "When I get my hands on them—" Another explosion rocked the mountain behind them.

The meadow wasn't that far away, but two big guys hiking uphill all the way, they were glad to get to the meadow, and some level ground. They stood at the top, right beside the meadow, and putting their hands on their knees, they bent over and caught their breath.

Immanuel hollered in the way he did, "Whoop, whoop, whoop!"

He trained all his horses to respect that holler, and Trevor came running. Trevor was Shadow's best friend, and he was right behind Trevor. The boys walked over to where they hid their tack, and got the horses saddled up and the bits in their mouths.

"Let's go see what the Sam Hill this is all about?" Immanuel said.

They rode back down toward the cabins. The explosions had stopped, and about halfway back, they started to hear rifle fire, big rifles—Hawkens.

"Ya suppose them damned fools are havin' a gunfight with themselves?" Uzziah asked.

"I have no idea, young son, but let's get to the ridge above the cabins and see," Immanuel said.

They rode to the ridge, tied both horses up in case there were more explosions, and Immanuel took out his spyglass and glassed the cabins. The rifle and pistol fire continued in the background.

"What ya see?"

Immanuel, looking disgusted, handed the glass to

Uzziah, who looked down upon what was left of their destroyed cabins.

Roscoe was hiding in the barn and shooting at someone up the hill from him. Benjamin was lying behind the dead body of his little horse, which he often had to dismount when he went uphill because of his mangirth. He was firing at a point which seemed to be exactly opposite of where Roscoe was firing. Whoever had those two varmints in a firefight had gotten them into an enfilade, and that spelled death for both men. Then they heard a voice shout out.

"Hey, ifn yer not Immanuel and Uzziah, stop firing on us, ya done kilt my horse, Mable, and I hate ya fer it, but there's a lot of money we could share ifn yer in the right mind to do so?" It was Benjamin's voice, and both Uzziah and Immanuel became almost physically ill thinking they had been betrayed now, not only by the scribbler, but evidently by Roscoe and Benjamin.

"That reward must be a whopper," Immanuel whispered to Uzziah, who nodded in agreement.

"Yeah, we split the thousand dollars four ways and that's two hundred fifty a piece," Roscoe's big voice bellowed from the barn.

"Where is Immanuel and Uzziah?" That was Max, the man who had become an instant hero when he rode the schooner over the falls with the whore.

"This don't make no sense atall?" Uzziah queried in a whisper.

"Well, money changes everybody, and it looks like the ones we thought was square ain't!" Immanuel whispered right on top of Benjamin's voice.

"They ain't here!" Benjamin shouted up to the one side of the enfilade.

"Acause they been blown to bits, right?" Frederick asked.

"Looks like we got the angle and the height to end this, let's maim both of 'em and go down and look 'em in the eyes when we send them to perdition," Immanuel said.

Uzziah thought that was a good idea. "I'll shoot off Benjamin's shooting hand, and when Roscoe comes out, one of us will surely get 'em," Uzziah said as he lowered his Hawken and took careful aim.

———

Benjamin was sure that the other two, he knew it was Max and Frederick, he'd recognized Max's voice, and he was sure they'd come around. They were the two laziest mountain men in the mountains, and with two hundred fifty dollars apiece, they could lie back for a long time.

Then, his hand just disappeared. It was there one minute, then at the end of his right arm, there was a bloody pulp.

Benjamin screamed bloody murder, grabbed his bandana, and started wrapping the stump at the end of his arm, when Roscoe ran from the barn and was cut down by what sounded like two shots. Roscoe lay still and didn't move, all the while Benjamin was screaming.

"Roscoe! Roscoe, speak to me, damn it!" Benjamin got up and ran to where Roscoe lay. "Ya done kilt him ya sons-a-bitches! Ya done kilt him!" Blood was dripping all over Roscoe's destroyed body. He'd been hit from two different directions with two 54-caliber Hawken slugs. His guts were lying down where one slug had torn out his middle, and his chest was all blown up and out of proportion. Roscoe had always been barrel-chested, but it looked like the stays had been broken from the barrel and the contents let go of.

Frederick came full of stealth from the one direction, the north, and Max, crouching low, ran a straight line from the south. Both men carried their reloaded Hawkens, and they had pistols in their other hands.

"Oh my God, we gots to go through these blown-up cabins to find Immanuel and Uzziah's bodies," Max said as he put his pistol away and rubbed his head.

"Ya kilt my partner!" Benjamin complained from his bleeding position on the ground.

"Shut the hell up, ya back stabbin', no good, sidewinder!" Frederick said.

The two of them, Max and Frederick, had picked up any weapons from around Benjamin.

"Help me, I's gonna bleed to death," Benjamin shouted.

"That would be too good fer ya," Max said and hit him in the face with the butt of his Hawken, knocking him out.

"Come on, let's get this over with," Frederick said, almost in tears.

"Ain't nothin' to get over," Immanuel said as he rode in on Trevor.

"What the hell, how'd ya get outta this mess?!?" Max almost bawled out.

"We say our prayers at night," Uzziah quipped.

Immanuel got off his horse and put a tourniquet on Benjamin's stump. "Ya messed him up somethin' good, partner," he said.

"So, do either of ya have any idea what this was all

about, what the hell brought this on!?!" Uzziah asked both the other mountain men.

"It's my fault," Frederick said.

"What?" Immanuel asked.

"I told 'im, don't show it to 'em, but he thought we all in this together and we should organize," Max said.

"Organize what?" Uzziah asked.

"Ya don't know, do ya?" Frederick asked. "We thought fer sure ya knew by now."

"Knew what!?!" Immanuel asked from his position, where he was heating up a heavy piece of metal, which he used when shoeing the horses. The fire hadn't been blown out, and the coffee was still sitting there, and so were the cups. "Y'all want some coffee?" Immanuel added.

Frederick and Max came out of the debris where they'd started to look for the remains of Uzziah and his partner.

They came over and poured straight from the pot into the two cups. Frederick handed Max a cup. "Did y'all want some? I got a cup in my saddlebags," he asked.

"No, I'm good," Uzziah said, turning the totally torn-up body of Roscoe over.

"Me too," Immanuel said.

Frederick took a section of a newspaper out of his vest and unfolded it. "Look at this, both of ya," he said.

Immanuel took it and stared. "What in the world, who would post this?" he asked, then handed it to Uzziah, who whistled.

"We're worth more dead than alive," Uzziah said. "But why would they—" he broke off, not knowing exactly what to say.

"Ya knew about Roscoe's Army record, right?" Frederick asked.

"Yeah, he was in the artillery," Immanuel said.

"Uh-huh, but he got the boot by the Army 'cause he blew up a bunch of his own troops, and it was only an exercise," Max said. "One drunken night, he told me and Frederick about it, and he was purty upset about it, but the way he talked 'bout it, I think it done somethin' to his head, seeing all those men he knew scattered all over for two hundred yards.

"He said they wanted to court-martial him fer what he'd done, blowin' up all his friends, but his buddy from back home, Benjamin, broke him outta the stockade. Roscoe thought ifn he had money, he could go somewhere down in Mexico and live like an unwanted man."

"But killin' us fer money, after all we'd been through and we been faraway neighbors for how many years, they got chere afore Uzziah," Immanuel said.

"*Money is the root of all evil*, don't it say that in the Good Book, Uzziah?" Max asked.

Uzziah corrected the scripture, "*For the **love** of money is the root of all evil*, 1st Timothy 6:10."

"I'm guessin' they loved it more than they did y'all," Frederick said. "What are we gonna do with him?" he asked and pointed out the unhanded Benjamin who lay knocked out.

"Well, first we're agonna keep him from dying," Immanuel said, and he took the flat piece of iron from the fire, it was red hot, and taking off the bandana that Benjamin had put on his stump he placed the sizzling metal against the end of Benjamin's arm, he came awake, screaming, smelling his burning flesh, then passed out.

"Whatcha want him alive fer?" Max asked.

"Gonna take him down to Vrain's and let them deal with 'em. Don't the territorial law come through there every once in a while?"

"First I ever heard of it," Frederick said.

"I don't think we should go anywheres near that trading post, Immanuel," Uzziah said. "Think about it," he added.

Immanuel looked at his partner, whom he'd almost lost. Hell, he'd almost lost his own life, that fool throwing the explosives around like that, thank the Lord they had the horses up on the high pasture, or who knows what would have happened? About that time, Jenny came down and brayed like the donkey she was, and everybody laughed.

"Besides," added Frederick, "what the hell the law gonna do, but collect the bounty hisself?"

"True that," Max said.

"How come you guys—"

"Don't go there, we's yer friends no matter what, we ain't got any demons make us do things that Christian folk wouldn't do," Frederick said.

"What he said," Max agreed.

———

Uzziah had seen a man at the courthouse in one of the counties in the Shenandoah Valley make a hanging noose. He had never forgotten it, and now he was busy, doing just that to the lariat he carried.

Immanuel had picked out a good tree limb from one of the denuded ponderosas that they had torn up with the dynamite.

157

Max had gone out to where Roscoe had been smart enough to tie up his horse and brought it back to the cabins, what was left of them.

"Can I ride Roscoe's horse, now that ya done kilt mine?" Benjamin asked.

"Fer a little while, I reckon," Immanuel said.

"Yeah, he's a goodun, lest I won't have to walk when the going gets tough," Benjamin said. Then, becoming more aware, he saw Uzziah making the thirteen knots in the hangman's noose.

"What the hell y'all fixin' on doin' to me?"

"Hangin' by yer goddamned neck till yer dead, Benjamin, what'd ya think we was gonna do, give a prize?" Immanuel asked.

"But you guys ain't the law, this ain't right we been neighbors fer years—"

"Shut up, backstabber!" Uzziah said from where he was sitting, making the noose.

"Uzziah, Uzziah, yer a man of God, ya can't let them do this to me!" Benjamin got up and was complaining.

"Sit yer arse back down, dead man," Immanuel said, and pushed him back down on the stump he'd been sitting on.

"I done lost my right hand, had it shot right off my body, don't ya think that's enough?"

"Deadman complainin'," was all Immanuel said.

When the noose was finished, Uzziah threw it over the big denuded limb of one of the ponderosas and tied it around the trunk. Then, they got Benjamin up on Roscoe's horse, and even with one hand gone, he put up a hell of a fight.

"Yer all goin' to hell fer doin' this, that's where yer

agoin'," he yelled as it took all four of them to get him up on his partner's horse, who did not like what was going on.

"Ya wanna die like the coward ya are, or do ya wanna go out like a damned man?" Immanuel yelled at him.

Benjamin stopped fighting them and started crying. "My ma lives in Columbus, Ohio, well down by the river, just south, will ya go see her, and tell her I died a brave man?" Benjamin asked.

"Ifn ya die like that, we surely will," Uzziah said, then added, "Promise, what's her name?"

"Loretta Stevens, I was oldest of all seven kids," Benjamin said as his tears dried up. Immanuel had seen something like this before when a man condemned to death finally got by the fact that he was really going to die, and he settled into his death real natural-like.

"Okay, we ain't gonna hit yer horse, ya just spur him outta here," Immanuel said after the noose was placed by Uzziah around his neck. Benjamin even leaned over so Uzziah could get it there.

"No, she don't like the spurs, Roscoe said, and won't ever take off fast, 'less she's scared, better fire off yer Hawken right behind her, that'd do the trick," he said, and before the last word had finished sounding, Immanuel shot off his Hawken, and then Roscoe's horse took off with Benjamin holding the reins and trying to hold her back, but she was out of there. The reins were ripped from his hands, and he swung there, choking badly. The fall from the runaway horse had not done the trick.

Uzziah saw what was happening, and that Benjamin's tongue was lolling out and turning blue, so he took an uphill run at the swinging, almost corpse, and jumped up and grabbed Benjamin around the chest, and with the weight of the two bodies, it did the trick. They could all hear the snap of the neck, but Uzziah could actually feel it, and it sent shudders through his body as he dropped to the ground beneath the now swinging corpse.

4

The main highway that passed by Patrick Gass's rural road was nearly empty of traffic this time of morning. Well, the road was well out of Baltimore proper, but there was a lone black carriage drawn by a single black horse. It wasn't traveling fast, nor was it traveling slow, just a dogtrot. When it got to the cutoff for Gass's private road, it made a turn down that road, which had been dirt the first time Poe had traveled it, but now it was macadam, and nicely done, Poe thought.

Harriet Gass was sitting in the front window where the light was best, and she was embroidering a baby blanket for her oldest daughter, who was with child. She looked up when she heard the jangle and tinkle of the tack on the carriage.

"Are you expecting anyone, mon cherie?" she yelled to Patrick, who was just down the hall in his office. His office faced the back of the property, as he preferred the view of the paddock area over the front of the house and the main road into Baltimore.

Patrick Gass didn't answer, but walked in and kissed the top of Harriet's head as he looked out. The carriage was almost at the house by now, and he recognized the man driving it.

"It's Poe!" Patrick said excitedly.

"Who?" Harriet asked, looking out at the man as he stepped from the carriage. She thought he looked familiar, but could not place him.

"The man who was investigating the whereabouts of my wayward son," Patrick said, going to the door. He opened it before Poe had an opportunity to knock.

"You saw me coming," Poe said.

"Yes, we don't get many visitors out here, and Harriet saw your carriage. Did you meet her last time?"

"No, remember you came to my house. I'd thought I'd return the favor, and visit you this time," Poe said. She reached out her hand. "Delighted to meet you, Mrs. Gass," Poe said, and he kissed the top of her hand.

"Please, call me Harriet," she said, blushing. "Not many are as gallant as you these days," she added.

"Beauty deserves its rewards," Poe said.

"My husband said you were a poet, and now I hear why," Harriet commented as she sat back down to her embroidery.

"You have news?" Patrick asked.

"Yes, but meaning no disrespect to you, Harriet, I think the news is best delivered simply to your husband," Poe said.

"I know all about his oldest boy, he's never tried to keep secrets from me," she said.

"An admirable trait, I find that secrets will out regardless, your husband is a wise man," Poe said.

Patrick Gass thought for a moment. He did not

want to startle his wife, and it seemed perhaps Poe had something of a sensitive nature to tell him. "Yes, yes, you don't mind, my darling, if we go to my office?"

"Certainly not." Although she was disappointed, she understood, besides, Patrick would tell her all about it once Poe left.

"I hope this isn't presumptuous of me," Poe said, and taking something from his cape, it was a book, he held it out toward Harriet Gass. "This is my first published book," he said, and she took it and looked at the cover. "And I've inscribed it," he added.

"Tamerlane and Other Poems," she read, then added, "Thank you, thank you, so very much."

"Believe me, they are minor poems. I am working on something now which will change everything for me, and my publisher, I hope," Poe said.

She opened the book as they walked the short distance down the hallway to Patrick's office. She heard the door shut and thought that a pity, she had ever so good hearing and had hoped to eavesdrop while they were talking.

"Please sit down," Patrick said, and Poe sat opposite the great oak desk, which was neatly piled with papers.

As Poe looked around, he saw framed pastoral paintings and some sculptures, one of a horse and one of a naked woman, which was tastefully done.

"So, what have you got for me?" Patrick asked.

"Quite a lot, I'm afraid. I hate to dump so much on you all at once."

"First, tell me, did Ginny enjoy the trip?"

"That's gracious of you to think of, yes, she actually loved St. Louis, and we both enjoyed the Creole cooking we found there. Although it is not New

Orleans, some of the cooking was actually better than we expected."

"Wonderful."

"She did not go to all the places where I gathered information about your son, and as it turns out, he is quite well-known and well-remembered there."

"What name does he go by? I imagine it's an Indian name?"

"His moniker is Immanuel James Jones, actually, and he wandered into the Growling Catfish, a saloon and sort of restaurant down by the docks. There, he befriended Uzziah Ferguson O'Bannon. They became fast friends, according to the owner, one Charles Watts. In fact, both shared a prostitute by the name of Sarah. There wasn't a last name for the young girl, if she ever had one. That part of St. Louis is depressed financially, economically, and there's very little law down by the docks even now.

"This friendship with the girl, Sarah, ended rather abruptly when an undersheriff by the name of Randall Hicken took the girl back to where those things of a carnal nature happen, and from all accounts from Watts, and the rest of the girls who work there, he opened her up like a mortician doing an autopsy."

"Good heavens!" Patrick exclaimed.

"The undersheriff later disappeared about the same time that your son Immanuel and his now partner, Uzziah, left town. There was a funeral for the girl right there in the consecrated grounds of Old St. Marcus Cemetery. There was an uproar over it, but when the pastors of the town were confronted with your son's Hawken rifle and the same make owned by Uzziah, they backed down.

"Watts told me that the undersheriff was standing up the hill from the ceremony and wearing, excuse my French, a shite-eating grin. Your son Immanuel and his partner Uzziah saw the man, and when they left town, the undersheriff was never seen again."

"So, where are they now?" Patrick asked.

"Let me show you these two items first," Poe said, and handed the article that Austin Fielder had written for the St. Louis Democrat.

"Read this," Poe said.

"Yes, well, it was picked up by the Baltimore papers, but now, I see, if my son is called Immanuel James Jones, then the article, which I've already read, was about him?!?"

"But I don't know if you've seen this." Poe handed him a dodger.

On it were drawings which Robert Spells had done of Immanuel and Uzziah when he was with them in the Rockies. Above both pictures, which were on the same dodger, it said, *Wanted: Dead or Alive $1,000 apiece.*

"How can this be? They didn't confess to doing this crime, did they?" Patrick asked.

"No, but the journalist Austin Fielder has sworn to the authorities that the story in the paper was told to him by your son, Immanuel," Poe said.

"But still, it's circumstantial at best," Patrick said.

"So, you know the law?" Poe asked.

"My eldest boy by Harriet, Montague Gass, is a lawyer, and I've seen him work in the courtroom," Patrick said.

"Yes, saying something happened doesn't mean it really did happen, but if the journalist has another witness to what your son told him, well, it goes from circumstantial to a confession of sorts, doesn't it?"

"But who would have heard the story, the confession?"

"His partner, Uzziah O'Bannon, if he were there, the prosecution could offer him a deal to stay off the gallows, if he backed Fielder's story," Poe said.

"My God," Patrick said.

"But as I am sure you are aware, that's not the real problem now. The real problem is that they are wanted for this crime, whether they did it or not, and wanted dead or alive. A thousand dollars apiece will inspire a lot of unsavory types to go after your boy, and I'm afraid if you don't find them first, then the rest is moot," Poe said.

"Well, how, I mean, the Rocky Mountains go all the way from Mexico to Canada!"

"Yes, but I did some more research. It seems the Pinkertons were on their trail both on the Missouri River, and later they chased them around Virginia, where Uzziah's parents have a farm."

"Do you know—"

"Yes, Uzziah's father's name is Sean O'Bannon, and I took the liberty of writing down the directions to his farm," Poe said as he handed Patrick Gass another envelope.

"How did you find all this information?"

"There was a story written in an Alexandria, Virginia, paper, The Gazette, about both your son and Uzziah. I found the reporter, Munford Baldwin, and he told me where the farm was, but I had to promise to get back in touch with him if anything developed."

"Seems to me, the press is the reason my boy and the O'Bannon boy are in trouble."

"There's responsible journalism, Mr. Gass, there is, it's just when a story is hot, everyone wants in on it, and I couldn't have gotten the information without making that promise," Poe said.

————

Sean O'Bannon and two of his sons, Hank and Raymond, were busy getting their horses all tacked up and stuffing supplies into saddlebags, and stacking the rest of them on a sawbuck saddle, which was sitting on a mule that kept braying every time a new item was added.

"Do ya think it's too much fer her, Pa?" Raymond asked. He was twenty-three years old, with black raven hair, well built, and one of his ma's favorites.

"Nah, she's just complainin' like every woman," Sean said.

"I heard that," Rahab, Sean's wife, said. She looked better since she'd gotten over her sickness when Uzziah was there. She gained some weight back and looked robust and rosy in the cheeks.

"Mama, ya know I was only talkin'—"

"Shite, yeah, I know, I've packed some biscuits and some sandwiches," Rahab said.

Sean kissed her.

"How in tarnation are ya gonna find Uzziah afore those men who want him dead?" she asked.

"By the grace of the Almighty God, that's how," Sean said, then added, "We're takin' a train from Richmond to St. Louis, then the paddle wheeler from there up the Missouri toward where that reporter said he got them to tell him their bloody story."

"It ain't gonna be like y'all be there tomorrow!"

"I know, I know, Mother, but we have to start some time, and this is when we're startin'," Sean said.

When he looked up, there were a couple of riders coming down the dirt road that led to the farm.

"Who d'ya suppose that'll be?" Raymond asked.

"Get Hank, in case there's trouble," Sean said, and Raymond went toward the barn where Hank was getting the guns ready.

The riders weren't exactly riding fast down the private farm road, and Hank had made it out from the barn before they arrived.

"Here's yer guns, Pa, and they's loaded," Hank said as he handed Sean a rifle and a pistol. Raymond was already armed.

"Hello the farm!" a voice rang out from one of the riders, the older one, it looked like.

Sean waved and shouted back, "Hello the riders!"

The two riders pulled up and sat their horses, seeing that there were horses being prepared for a journey, and also a packed mule.

"I'm Patrick Gass, and this is my son, Monty Gass. Are you the parents of Uzziah O'Bannon?"

Sean looked at Rahab and his two boys, and several other children began to spill from the big farmhouse. "You kids, get back inside, now!" Sean yelled, and they obeyed.

"Please, don't be frightened, I am the father of Immanuel James Jones. I believe you've met my son?"

Sean and his older boys relaxed. "What do ya want?" Sean asked, still skeptical.

"Well, looks like you're getting ready to go find your boy, we'd like to come along," Gass said.

"Get on down and let's talk," Rahab said, and they went into the house.

Once it was discovered that both parties were thinking in exactly the same way, and that by the grace of the Almighty, Immanuel's pa had shown up exactly when they were getting ready to leave, Rahab knew that this was a sign. It ain't often that you know when God was at work, but surely this was one of those times.

"I think yer mission will be a success," she said, then added, "When Father wants things to succeed, he often intervenes, and I can see no other reason why you two would be here just as my husband and two eldest sons are about to embark on the same mission."

Patrick Gass listened, and he didn't want to be disrespectful, but he put their meeting like this down to the fine work that Edgar Allan Poe had done for him. He and Monty had started out west for the Virginia farm the same day Poe delivered the news.

"I have no doubt that you are right," Monty said, knowing as any lawyer does, that it was best to agree with those on the same side, regardless of what they were saying, as long as they had the same objective.

5

U zziah and Immanuel felt that it was stupid to stay at their cabins, since just about everyone at the Vrain Trading Post, and a lot of other folks, knew exactly where those cabins were. They buried Roscoe and Benjamin the same day, and with the four of them digging, it didn't take long.

They decided that they would bury their bodies where they had lived as mountain men. It seemed most appropriate.

"Where do we go from here?" Uzziah asked, wiping the dirt off his hands. His mind had been occupied with Benjamin and how he had helped the man die. He couldn't get the shudder of the dying man's body off his mind. He'd tried to talk to Immanuel, and his response had been typical Immanuel. *"Ya put him down like a horse with a broken leg, ya done the man a favor, hell, I was happy with just watching the bastard choke to death!"*

Immanuel looked at his partner for all these years. Uzziah had surprised him when he jumped on

Benjamin's body to help break his neck. Heck, he didn't think the young son had it in him. And now, his partner wanted to know where they'd go from there? Immanuel wasn't sure, he just wasn't.

"Partner, yer guess is as good as mine," Immanuel said, looking at Uzziah, Max, and Frederick at the same time.

"Well, ya can't stay at yer cabins, too many people that know ya know where ya live," Frederick said.

"That's a fer sure," Uzziah said, "but where?"

"How 'bout down where Standing Bear lives, the settlement?" Max asked.

"It'll put her and the children in too much danger," Uzziah said immediately.

"Don't discount that immediately," Immanuel said. "After all, we could send a pigeon down there and explain things."

"Ya think she knows?" Max asked.

"Hey, didn't think anybody knew till we was being blown up," Immanuel said.

———

They went back to the cabins, and they were a wreck. There was maybe one cabin that still looked like it could be occupied. The work that the two mountain men had done on the potbellied cabin was all undone, the stove had been blown clear off into the woods, they like to never found it. Luckily, the tumbler pigeons were fine. They were on the back of the barn, and only part of the barn had been destroyed. Besides, they left the coop door open all the time, and at the first explosion, they must have headed for the hills. Now, back in the coop, they were fairly anxious and fluttering all around.

"Ya think they'll do what they're supposed to do?" Immanuel asked Uzziah.

"They're homing pigeons. They don't go back to Standing Bears 'cause they want to, they go back because it's in their brains! They have to, and believe me, after all that's happened up here, they're probably ready as hell to get out of here!"

"Hope yer right," Immanuel said.

"We'll send a message, see 'bout the lay of the land down there, and wait for an answer for—how long does it usually take?"

"No more than two—three days," Uzziah said.

"We'll hide out up in the big pasture till then," Immanuel said.

"We'll go with ya," Max said.

"What 'bout yer hoochie mama?" Immanuel asked, he was so indelicate sometimes.

"Oh, yer talkin' 'bout Anabelle, the girl who said I'd be her hero for all time?"

"Yeah, the one ya went over the falls with and who said she loved ya," Immanuel reminded him.

"Yeah, well—"

"It's hard fer him to talk 'bout it," Frederick said. "She was fine fer a while, but the winter sorta made her a bit crazy—"

"A bit crazy, she came at me with a gall dern knife, she did!" Max said, and all three of the other mountain men chuckled.

"Cabin fever comes in all varieties," Immanuel said.

"Yeah, well, that variety can get ya kilt," Max said.

"I done took her ass down to Vrain as soon as spring showed its beautiful head."

"So, we'll be up in the meadow, ya know the one, fer two days, then we'll be back down chere," Uzziah said.

"Nah," Frederick said. "We's gonna go witcha, no sense in reducing yer numbers when ya might have another fight, or two, on yer hands."

They agreed. Uzziah wrote the note, and Immanuel told him what he wanted in it, and they let the tumbler go. He circled the mountain cabin a few times, tumbling away, then took off east and south.

All four of them went up and camped in the high meadow.

"We shouldn't camp together, in case there's trouble, the other party can come to the rescue," Immanuel said, and the two other mountain men seemed a bit put off by their friends not camping with them. Uzziah thought they had been looking forward to his cooking. They had brought Jenny up with them and all the supplies that weren't spoiled.

———

While he was making supper that night, Uzziah turned to Immanuel. "Ya don't trust 'em, do ya?"

Immanuel looked over to where, about a half mile away, the other campfire was smoking. "I hate to say it, partner, but the amount of money on our heads is makin' me doubt just 'bout everything."

"Well, I made 'nuff fer 'em to eat with us, ride over and tell 'em supper's ready, will ya?"

Immanuel rode over, and when he was a bit from

their camp, they got all spooked and were up with their guns as Immanuel rode in.

"Dinner's ready," Immanuel said, noticing that there was nothing on their fire, and they were chomping on jerked meat.

"No kiddin'!" Max said and was on his horse before Frederick and riding toward Uzziah's fire.

"That boy does love yer partner's grub," Frederick said.

"Who don't!?" Immanuel agreed.

———

It worked like that for the next two days. Uzziah would cook, and the other two, Frederick and Max, would ride over and eat with them. Immanuel began to feel it was stupid that he was keeping the two camps separated until the evening of the third day, when they would ride down and check on the tumblers. It was way past sunset when Uzziah happened to hear something.

"Immanuel, there's somebody down near the other camp," he whispered.

"What?"

"Shhh!" Uzziah pointed down to where Frederick and Max had gone to sleep for the night.

Immanuel got his spyglass out and glassed their camp, and there were two other horses down there. The men down there weren't getting off their horses, and they had guns on the two other mountain men.

Immanuel grabbed up his Hawken, and Uzziah followed suit. They had their saddles there and used them as supports for their rifles.

"Can ya see good enough?" Uzziah asked.

"Not really," Immanuel said, and that was when the fire down there got bigger, evidently, one of them had thrown something else on the fire, they must have known.

"Good as gold now," Immanuel whispered and counted to three, and both men squeezed off their shots at the same time.

———

Down at Max and Frederick's camp, the talk was getting harsh.

"We ain't gonna ask another time. Ifn ya ain't Uzziah and Immanuel, then where are they!?!" the youngest of the two asked. He was probably in his early twenties and not a mountain man. His partner was older and nervous and most likely got talked into this by the young one.

"Hey, we're up here all by our lonesome, fellas," Frederick said.

"That's not what Anabelle said, she said you two and the two wanted are fast as thieves, and ifn we found ya, we'd find them?" the young one said.

"That a fact? How is Anabelle anyway?" Max asked as he tossed a bit of drier wood on their fire, hoping that Immanuel and Uzziah were paying attention.

"What'd ya do that fer?" the older one said as he looked around in the deepening twilight.

"It's cold, case ya haven't noticed," Max said.

"Well, yer whore said ya had some mistaken idea about her, she said—" that was the last word the young one got out before his side exploded, the older one saw that, then his head was blown off. Blood was everywhere when Frederick and Max heard the two shots.

"Damnation! Good shootin'!" Max yelled as he stood up, hollered, and waved toward Immanuel and Uzziah's camp.

———

They took off that very night. They went down to their cabin and they could tell, the two who had just died, that they did not bury, had been there. Stuff was thrown around, but the pigeons were fine.

There was a tumbler there with a message from the settlement on it.

It seemed Standing Bear didn't give a shite what trouble they were in, she said she'd sent for help and to come on down.

They took off for the settlement right away, but did not take the direct route. They circled around, watching their backtrail closely just in case others had been with the two dead men.

A day and a half later, they circled the settlement, and when they came up to the stockade gate, Uzziah hollered in.

"Hello the settlement!" he yelled. The others had stayed back in the trees, just in case.

There was a holler like an Injun, and for just a minute, Uzziah was about to ride out of there, but when the gate was opened, there was Beckwourth all dressed like a Crow and sitting around various fires. There must have been twenty to twenty-five Crow braves, and they were painted up like they were a war party, even Beckwourth.

Uzziah wasn't sure what to do as Immanuel and the other two mountain men rode up.

"What the hell's goin' on!?!" asked Max.

It was supper, and they had supper with Beckwourth, Standing Bear, Leah, Willet, and the kids. Boy, Uzziah couldn't believe how much the kids had grown. Willy and Charlie looked like little men, and Cubby was dressed in Crow dress, and he must have been nearly five years old. He spoke perfect Crow to them.

"Ya hear that, Immanuel, the kid speaks perfect Crow!" Uzziah remarked.

"So, I am Crow," Cubby said in English, and he looked every bit like his pa, Oscar.

"I taught him both, since he is sorta both," Standing Bear said.

"Aren't you my grandfather? Where have you been?" Cubby asked, wanting to go to Immanuel but holding back.

"Come here, Cubby, grandpa loves ya," Immanuel said in Crow to the boy, and he ran into Immanuel's arms.

"I seen the dodger on ya," Beckwourth said. "Did ya really tell that reporter yer story, or is he full of shite?"

Immanuel looked to the ground.

"He done told the story, but it's only half the story," Uzziah said, trying to save face for Immanuel.

"So, what do we do now?" Beckwourth asked in Crow.

"We?" Immanuel asked in Crow.

"We!" There came a voice from the door, and there stood the Crow medicine man's son, who had been the buffalo runner.

Immanuel turned, and the man who was no longer

a boy came up to him, and they shook arms the way the Crow did. "My name is now, Buffalo Warrior," he said in Crow.

"A perfect name," Immanuel said back in Crow. "But what do you have to do with my troubles?" Immanuel asked in Crow.

"Your troubles are mine, as mine are yours," Buffalo Warrior said. "You came for me when I was taken, and now, I am here for you and your partner."

"Here's the plan," Beckwourth said in English, and the two mountain men sat at the table and were served supper as Beckwourth explained how they were going to get from the settlement to safety without any incidents.

———

Patrick Gass and his son Monty rode with Sean and his two sons, Raymond and Hank, from the train station in St. Louis and toward the docks where they hoped to make a rapid connection with a paddle wheeler to Mandan territory. They would make inquiries there about the whereabouts of their sons, Immanuel and Uzziah. Their best bet, they both agreed, was the Catholic Black Robe that had written Patrick the letter.

These were times when a man wished he could fly like a bird to be of help to their sons, but travel was travel, and it all took time. They had made good connections from Richmond to St. Louis, and only once were they challenged when they realized that the train they had transferred to did not have the stockcar connected to it that had their horses and supplies on it. They had to make a lot of fuss, and finally, the right stockcar was brought and hooked up. But other than that, the trip had been a time when two fathers, who never, ever expected to meet each other, had the opportunity to talk, gamble, break bread together, and it seemed their sons had more in common than they had first expected.

Although Monty was a lawyer and a good one at that, Raymond had always wanted to study law, and Monty told him that when and if he wanted, all he had to do was come to his office in Baltimore, and he could apprentice with him. Hank was surprised that his younger brother, Raymond, had such leanings, but sometimes, the meeting of like minds brought things out in other people that families could never imagine.

It took them three days to get a paddle wheeler up the Missouri, and once they had settled into their rooms and made sure that their stock had been brought onboard, they settled into the rapid travel up the Mighty Mo. They ate dinners together, gambled against each other, and as it turned out, Sean had gambled some in his earlier life, before meeting Rahab, and he was winning a lot of money off Patrick, who could have cared less.

"Pa, does Ma know you're a card shark?" Monty asked his father one night as they sat out on the deck and watched the sunset.

"No, and ifn ya tell her, I'll have yer hide," Sean had said.

"Pa, I'm a grown man."

"Don't mean I won't give ya a beatin'," Sean had said.

Monty just laughed and got up and got them two more whiskeys. His pa was being very different, even talking different, and he sort of enjoyed this new version of the man who fathered him. It gave him a hint about the days when Patrick Gass, the carpenter, was with Lewis and Clark and had traveled this way before there were modern conveniences such as the paddle wheeler.

———

It was the morning of the next day that Hank was out on the deck after breakfast, and he heard a commotion coming from the other side of the ship. Running over, there were people pointing to a group of Injuns who were riding in the opposite direction as them, right beside the river, toward St. Louis.

"Oh my God," one man said, with binoculars held to his face. "They got four White men as captives!"

"May I?" Hank asked the man with the binocs.

"Sure, son, have a look, sure wouldn't wanna be them four!" he said as he handed the binoculars to Hank.

Hank looked and couldn't quite believe his eyes!

"Hey, Pa, come here!" he yelled to Sean, who was having breakfast with Patrick Gass and the other boys.

"Can't it wait?"

"No, it cannot!" Hank said, then added to the man, "My pa's gotta see this."

The man nodded in agreement.

"What is it?" Sean asked Hank.

"Do ya mind?" he asked the man who was glassing the Injuns again.

"No, no, take a look! Seems like four of our brothers are in a bit of trouble," the man said as he handed the binocs to Sean.

Sean looked, yes, there were a lot of Injuns, and they seemed to be led by a Black man, but the really interesting thing was there were four men in the middle of the twenty-some Injuns, and they were dressed like Uzziah and Immanuel had been dressed when they came to visit Rahab when she was sick.

"My God, son, that can't be Uzziah and Immanuel! Hey, Patrick, ya gots to see this!" Sean yelled to Patrick.

The paddle wheeler captain had been convinced, well there was the matter of the money which Patrick had offered him, but reluctantly he pulled the paddle wheeler to the southern bank of the Missouri, and Patrick Gass, Monty, Sean and his two sons, Hank and Raymond, rode their horses, all with their pack mules off the loading deck and onto the prairie.

6

To say that this was an unusual formation of both Crow and white man would be understating what it was by a bunch. The Crow warriors had war paint on their faces, and feathers in their hair, and even Buffalo Warrior had a war bonnet, and Beckwourth, who had been a war chief of the Crow for many years. Riding with them, of course, were his four wives, and naturally, Standing Bear wasn't going to let anything like this come out of her compound without her being a part of it—ever!

Uzziah looked over at the two of them, Immanuel and Standing Bear. There wasn't a better sight anywhere. She was proud, and considering what she had been through and how she had recovered, she had every right to be so.

Immanuel was his cocky, old self, and the way he'd done up his hair, well, some of Beckwourth's wives had helped him, he had fetchers braided into his long locks, and the wind was blowing his long hair back off his shoulders, and he'd changed his old hat for a buckaroo, which one of the Crow had found on the plains, and had traded Immanuel for it. Immanuel had given the buck some trinkets that he'd had for a long time, which didn't mean much to him, but the thing that turned the trick was an old scalp which Immanuel had Trevor wear on his bridle. The Crow wanted that scalp above all else, and Immanuel figured trading someone's top knot for a top-shelf buckaroo hat was a good deal. Both the Crow warrior and Immanuel felt they'd gotten the best out of the deal, and that's what good trading was all about!

Uzziah had allowed a few feathers, mostly hawk and eagle, to be braided into his hair, but he still wore the old slouch hat that he had favored since he left Virginia. It was odd how a man could start wearing something, then after a time, that something—either because of the time you had on it, or just plain superstition, it was the hat you were wearing when you almost lost your life, etc.—didn't make much difference before you started feeling like it just might be your lucky hat.

Of course, their ever-present Hawkens were across their laps, one hand on their reins and the other on the Hawken.

Uzziah wished that there was a magic way for this moment to be caught in time, but the camera obscura, which was in its infancy, could not catch such things because the subjects had to remain still for a long time, and this rollicking, swaying band of warriors, both red and white, was something that you almost had to smell, taste, breath to get the idea of its majesty.

One of the Crow who was riding in the back of the war party had seen dust rising up behind the party of twenty-some Crow and four mountain men. He had ridden right up to Buffalo Warrior and told him.

"Go back and see what it is, how many, then come back," Buffalo Warrior had told him, and the Crow cut out of the group and rode toward their backtrail.

"What's going on?" Immanuel asked Buffalo Warrior in Crow.

"Maybe trouble, I don't know. Brave will soon return with what he sees," Buffalo Warrior told Immanuel.

"What's up?" Uzziah asked Immanuel.

"Somebody's on our backtrail," Immanuel told him.

"Well, they gots to be on the baddest backtrail that anyone ever got on," Max said. He had never felt this protected in his entire life out on the prairie.

"That's a fer sure," Frederick agreed. He and his partner hadn't liked the idea of traveling with a Crow war party, but when Immanuel explained about the history that Buffalo Warrior and the rest of the Crow had with them, he and Uzziah, it seemed to put the other two mountain men at ease. Still, both of them had to pinch themselves from time to time. In any other life on this particular planet, in this particular solar system, they would be dead on the prairie and their scalps taken.

Immanuel rode up alongside Buffalo Warrior.

"Say, where's yer brave goin'?" he asked.

"There's some White men on our trail, they might be after the monies for your scalps," Buffalo Warrior said.

Immanuel thought about that, and since he was the only man that he knew of on this trail who had a spyglass, he kicked Trevor up into a run out of the formation, and when Uzziah saw Immanuel leave the safety of the group, he just had to break from it, too, and see what was happening.

It became evident to Buffalo Warrior and the rest of the party that they weren't protecting anyone since who they were protecting had just broken from their security and ridden back with the Crow scout. Buffalo Warrior yelled something in Crow and the whole column made the turn with Max and Frederick inside it.

Uzziah had no trouble catching up with Immanuel because of Shadow's speed, and the two of them saw at the same time the one scout on top of a knoll which overlooked the trail they had been on. They rode up, jumped off their horses, leaving them ground tied, and crawled up beside the Crow scout.

"Can you see them?" Immanuel asked in Crow, and the scout pointed toward the horizon. Immanuel took out his spyglass and zeroed in on the five White men. He took the spyglass from his eye, rubbed his eye, and put it back.

"What's ya lookin' at?" Uzziah asked him.

"Well, it just can't be!" Immanuel said.

"Who is it?"

"It looks a lot like your pa, Sean, and two of yer brothers, can't recall their names."

Uzziah took the spyglass from him and focused in on the riding White men. "It is my pa, and my brothers Raymond and Hank, but ain't got no ideation who the othern are," Uzziah said, then added, "Let's ride down and greet them."

"Don't think we'll have a chance to beat the rest of the Crow down there," Immanuel said, looking over his shoulder.

———

Sean O'Bannon and his sons, Hank and Raymond, were kicking their horses up so they could find the band of Injuns who had taken Uzziah and Immanuel captive. Patrick Gass and Monty were right with them, but no one had determined what they might do, besides die along with Immanuel and Uzziah.

"Here they come!" shouted Hank from his saddle, and the others saw now in the distance, the band of warriors with their ponies painted and their hair adorned with feathers.

As the Crow got closer, the five White men slowed their horses, and it seemed to Standing Bear that they were searching with their eyes for Immanuel and Uzziah. Perhaps these men were nothing but scalp hunters, and they all deserved to die, she thought as the band of twenty-some Crow and two White men surrounded them.

"Where's Uzziah?" one of the men asked.

"And Immanuel, where's the other two White men?" Patrick asked.

"Ya talkin' 'bout usin," Max asked, sounding about as illiterate as any man could.

"I can see you're White, but—" Sean had to stop because he could see riding from the other side of a knoll, the two White men they were looking for.

"Here they come now," he said to Patrick, and all the White men stood in their stirrups and looked at the coming party. Mistaking that movement and their seeing Immanuel and Uzziah as a threat, one Crow brave shot an arrow into Hank's chest just above his heart.

There were shouts from the Crow band, and no more arrows flew, as Hank fell from his horse and Sean and Raymond were at his side.

Patrick drew his pistol, but one of the men in the riding hard party shouted out something. "If ya shoot they'll kill each and every one of ya!" Uzziah shouted as he rode up.

———

They had Hank on his back on the ground. Immanuel was down beside him. Hank was conscious, but in a lot of pain.

"That there arrow can't come out the way it went in, son," Immanuel said.

"What ya mean?" Hank asked, not knowing what was coming.

Quick introductions had been made, and now, Patrick was standing behind his eldest boy, Immanuel, and watching and listening to everything he said and did.

"Anybody got any whiskey?" Immanuel asked, and of course, Uzziah had a bottle in his saddlebag. He'd taken to bringing one wherever they went because of Immanuel's habit.

"Like ya didn't know," Uzziah said, handing the bottle to his partner.

"Ya a drinker, Hank?"

"A bit now and then, mostly at Thanksgiving," Hank said through bated breath.

Immanuel uncorked the bottle and took a healthy drink.

"I thought that was for Hank!?" Sean asked.

"It is, but someone's got to do what I got to do, and I ain't doin' it without a couple stiff ones," Immanuel said. "So, Hank, tilt this chere soldier up and let's kill him together."

"Huh?" Hank asked, befuddled by the whole linguistic turn.

"We're gonna take turns and empty this bottle as fast as we can, ya got it?"

"That'll make me drunk," Hank protested.

"Yeah, that's the idea," Immanuel said and put the bottle to Hank's lips, and some of it came from the corners of his mouth, but he swallowed a lot.

"Good man, now my turn." Immanuel pretended to drink heavily from the bottle, but Uzziah could see that the level was staying the same as his partner put the bottle back to Hank's lips, and he swallowed quite a bit, then choked.

"Sorry, ain't used to...wow, things are spinnin'," Hank said, and Immanuel laughed.

"Good, good." Immanuel tilted the bottle again, and didn't really, hardly take any, and back to Hank's mouth again, and the boy seemed to be getting the hang of it, and when the bottle was taken away, there was barely a corner left.

"Somebody pick this drunk up, will ya, just sit him up," Immanuel asked.

Sean got behind Hank and pushed him to a sitting position, and before anyone had a chance to react, Immanuel slugged Hank hard across the jaw, his head snapped to the side, and he was out.

"What'd ya do that fer!" Sean was hot.

"Just stay behind him and keep him off the dirt,"

Immanuel said as he poured half of what was left on the entrance wound and saved the rest.

"Hold 'im tight, everybody, get down and grab his legs, ifn he wakes, we'll have hell to pay," Immanuel said as he took his left hand, placed it on the feathered end of the arrow, and broke it off. "Uzziah, hand me my gloves," Immanuel said, then, putting them on, pushed with both hands on the arrow as it began to move through Hank's body.

They could see the arrow making its way deeper into his body—

"Aren't ya harming him?" Sean asked.

"No, ain't nothin' between this entrance and his back meat," Immanuel said, grunting as he pushed the arrow through.

Monty Gass lost consciousness and fell to the prairie floor. The others made their own sounds of pain, which were merely empathetic.

When the arrow was far enough out of Hank's back, Immanuel reached around and pulled the broken shaft all the way through. He covered the exit wound now with whiskey, then he took the herbs that Uzziah had prepared over the fire and placed them on both wounds, then, taking the gauze from Uzziah bound both wounds by stretching the gauze around Hank's body.

"Can't ride no horse," he said in English, then said in Crow to Buffalo Warrior, "Send braves to make a travois."

"Already here," Buffalo Warrior said in Crow as two braves rode up with the travois. "Crows know what to do," he added proudly.

They placed Hank on the travois and began again

in the manner in which they had been traveling. It was slower going, but when they camped that night, Standing Bear nursed Hank O'Bannon, who had come around. When Standing Bear left to get Hank dinner, he signaled to his brother, Uzziah.

"What's ya need?" Uzziah asked, squatting down by the travois, which had been unhooked from Hank's horse.

"Where did that angel come from?" Hank asked, looking toward Standing Bear.

"She's a friend of ours from a place called the settlement," Uzziah said.

"That's where I'm movin' when all this is done with," Hank said, taking his brother's hand.

"Okay, you can do that," Uzziah said, "but that angel was in hell before she got to heaven."

"Kinda figured with her being White, and dressin' like that, what happened?"

"When yer better, ask her, she'll probably tell ya, if she don't kill ya," Uzziah said, chuckling.

"What?" Hank said, then noticed she was coming back with his supper. "Here she comes," he added.

"Yep, that's her, fer sure," Uzziah said. "Enjoy yer meal," he added.

"Thanks for taking care of my brother Hank," Uzziah said in Crow to Standing Bear.

"He looks like you, very handsome and a bit younger," Standing Bear said, smiling.

"Well, ya done took his heart," Uzziah said in Crow.

"Then, I will treat it with tenderness," she said back to Uzziah in Crow.

As she was feeding Hank, a Crow warrior came

over and kneeled down on the other side of Standing Bear and was whispering to her.

"He is the one who shot you," Standing Bear said to Hank.

"Couldn't have told, didn't see nothin' just felt the arrow," Hank said, and Standing Bear translated his reply to the Crow warrior, who smiled and said some more to her in muted tones.

"He wants you to know that he regrets acting without thinking, he was only trying to protect the Wolverine."

"Who's the Wolverine?"

"That's the name the Crow have come up with for Uzziah. They say he looks cuddly when he's not angry, but when he bares his teeth, he will tear whoever opposes him to shreds."

"Does Uzziah know that's what they call him?" Hank asked.

Standing Bear said something in Crow to the warrior and they both laughed. "No, he does not, he thinks of himself as a bear, but a wolverine is harder to shoot, and impossible to kill, so they do him a great honor in this naming."

That night after supper, as the White men sat around one fire and the Crow around another, the Crow had done their own cooking and, of course, Uzziah had cooked for the others. Pipes were pulled out, and the conversation of all conversations was about to begin.

"So, tell me again, Immanuel, why exactly are you

going to the place where they have a murder warrant out for your arrest and Uzziah's?" Patrick asked.

"So, ya really did come lookin' fer me after the Sioux took me?"

"Yeah, of course, your Mandan mother must have told you that, right?"

"I reckon, but maybe I didn't quite believe it," Immanuel said. "It's gonna take me a bit to really think of ya as my pa, but I'll come around."

"So, Uzziah, is this the way he answers questions, with something that has nothing to do with the question you asked?" Patrick asked, and Uzziah chuckled.

"Yeah, sounds about right, go ahead, partner, tell yer pa our reasonin'," Uzziah said and threw a smoking twig out of the fire at Immanuel.

Immanuel grabbed it and put it out completely. "Okay, Pops, mind ifn I call ya Pops?"

"Hey, just finding you is amazing, so I'm a little concerned that you'd want to trunk yourselves in for such a serious charge?"

"It's like this, Pops, before, when we knew we was wanted, well, that was one thing that we could do a work-around on, but this new bounty and the dodgers which were sent out just about everwheres, well, we done lost most of our cabins, we had friends turn their backs on good sense and try to collect, and dealing with them, well, let me tell ya, that was rough," he said and looked at Uzziah, who still could feel the shudder that went through the body of Benjamin when he helped him to his death.

"Anyway, we just thought, there's no sense in waiting for the inevitable, some hardcase is gonna find us when we're in our unawares, collect somethin' he never should have collected."

"It was face the music time, Patrick, that's all it was," Uzziah added.

"Well, I sent an investigator out to St. Louis, and after his reconnoitering, he assures me that this case is a *he-said-she-said* kind of thing. And according to this man, who is very insightful, these sorts of conflicts are circumstantial, since opposing parties have differing opinions and there is no concrete evidence."

"Well put, Pops, are ya sure ya ain't a lawyer?" Immanuel asked.

"Pa's thinking is following the reasoning of Edgar Allan Poe. Do you know his writings?"

"Ain't he the one with all the sort of macabre stories?" Sean asked.

"That's right, his *Murders of the Rouge Morgue* was what caught my attention," Patrick said.

"The monkey did it!" Sean exclaimed.

"Well, it was an orangutan, but yes, a member of the primate species did it," Patrick said.

"Ya know, Uzziah, yer ma Rahab read that story to me when we was getting ready to go to sleep, like to give me the heebie-jeebies," Sean said. "Couldn't get to sleep after I heard it!"

"Yes, yes, but don't you see, Poe created a detective, a Monsieur Dupin, who came up with a method, really for his own amusement, whereby things which seemed unsolvable could be solved. He called it ratiocination, which is nothing but the process of exact thinking. It's surprising how many people don't think logically," Patrick finished up.

"So, Pops, ya think ya can base our defense on

nothin' more than a guy who makes things up about monkeys and has 'em published?"

"I know it sounds sketchy, but how were you going to defend yourselves in a court of law?" Patrick asked, and everyone around the fire looked at the two mountain men.

"We's just gonna tell 'em, we didn't do it!" Immanuel said.

"But, partner, we did do it!" Uzziah said.

And the silence around the campfire was deafening.

"That is the last time I want you to say anything like that, you understand?" Patrick warned. "I mean, unless you want to be hung by the neck until dead?" Patrick's question was met with guffaws from those around the campfire, but Uzziah remembered Benjamin's shuddering body, and his skin went cold.

"You okay, partner?" Immanuel asked, for he could tell that since the hanging, Uzziah had been a bit reserved, and maybe, just maybe, he was thinking about confessing.

"Yeah, I'm fine," Uzziah said.

"Ya can't confess, ifn ya confess, then I'll be hangin' next to ya on the gallows," Immanuel pleaded.

"Who said I's gonna confess shite. Truth be told, we did the whores of St. Louis a favor and ridded the world of a mean and horrible man," Uzziah said.

"And do I have to remind you again, Uzziah, all this talk has to stop before we get to St. Louis, understand?" Patrick was adamant now.

"Yes, sir," Uzziah said, and it sounded like he meant it.

———

That night, when everybody was turning in and guards had been posted by the Crow braves who would put up with no shite at all, Immanuel came to where Uzziah was settled into his bedroll.

"We gotta talk," Immanuel said.

"Shoot."

"We committed murder, in a sense, I mean the man was alive when we left him, and I guess ya could say, the varmints finished him off. This is not the time to weigh yer soul before yer God, understand?"

"He's yer Father, too. One day we will stand in judgment," Uzziah reminded his partner.

"Yeah, but not in a St. Louis courtroom, okay. Judgment day, I'll be willin' and able to stand afore God and look him right in the eye and say I done what I done, but God's God, and the judge in St. Louis is the judge in St. Louis, do not get the two confused, young son, do not!"

Uzziah looked at Immanuel. "You are my partner, and a man I hold in high regard, heck, I love yer nasty ass, but let me deal with Father the way I deal with him. I won't bring ya down and I won't confess, all I got to do is remember what her body looked like when we found her whose name we cannot speak. I will never forget that it was you who sewed her back together so she could fit in that coffin and it was you and I who stood up to those pious-assed pastors who didn't want her buried in sanctified ground," Uzziah said and grabbed his partner's arm and they held their arms like that for a bit, and Immanuel, satisfied, went back to his bedroll.

7

It could be said that the city of St. Louis was not ready for what happened because, simply, they were not. As it was happening, the then mayor of St. Louis, the Honorable John D. Daggett, sent a boy on a fast horse toward Jefferson Barracks Military Post. It was a scant ten and a half miles away, and the boy was a good rider. Still, it would take at least twenty minutes to get there, then the boy would have to explain about the situation, then the Commander, Brevet Major Stephen W. Kearny, would have to assemble troops and make the trip back to St. Louis. There simply wouldn't be enough time.

They, the entire group of Crows and the nine White men with them, were spotted by a group of people who were down by the Missouri River where it passes by the city. They reported that a group of war-painted Injuns had swam the Missouri on their horses, and that there appeared to be White men in the middle of the Injuns, and all of them were headed for the center of town.

The sheriff of St. Louis was down by the Missouri shortly after that, but missing the group by a good fifteen minutes. He followed their tracks into the city, where a panic was started unadvisedly by people screaming and running for cover. It was later reported that some men had thought about firing on the group, but had decided it was better if they simply hid.

When they got to the courthouse, which was a stately building with a fine cupola and large chambers for the courts on either side of the main rotunda, they were but a few hundred yards from the Mississippi River.

"All you Crows wipe off your war paint, we don't want anybody to get the wrong idea," Immanuel said in Crow, and fairly soon all the war paint was gone from their faces, but their war ponies stayed painted, and the feathers and braided hair stayed.

"Good thinking," Uzziah said to his partner. "Now what?"

"We wait for the authorities," Immanuel said.

The White men, all nine of them, had more or less separated themselves from the Crow, but were still in the middle of the circle of the Crow braves.

Within less than ten minutes, riders appeared coming from the direction that Immanuel's party had taken after fording the Missouri, and they looked official. Uzziah saw several chests with badges on them, and their expressions were anything but friendly.

One man rode forward, but just about every other person in that group, probably ten men, had rifles pointed at the Crow Indians, which meant that they were pointed at the White men, also.

"What's the meaning of this, this, rabble-rousing

party?" the man asked. He was tall, and his stirrups were close to the ground. His bushy mustache had flecks of gray throughout, and it reminded Immanuel of a comment he'd heard once, when a man with such a large mustache had entered a gambling establishment out in Kansas.

The roulette operator said to the man, "Ya gonna eat that squirrel or just keep chewing on it!"

Immanuel decided not to say that, since the roulette operator was shot dead by the man two seconds later.

Uzziah and Immanuel walked to the front of their group right in front of the man on the horse.

"We come to turn ourselves in, we's wanted, Sheriff!" Uzziah said.

"I'm the mayor of St. Louis, John Daggett," he said.

"Please to meet ya, but, why's all them badges on those men with ya?" Uzziah asked, and Immanuel just looked at him.

"Those men are my private security," the mayor said.

"Well, these Crows are our private security," Immanuel said, not wanting to be outdone.

"What fer?" asked the mayor.

"What fer what?" Immanuel asked.

"What ya wanted fer?" Mayor Daggett asked.

"Fer the murder of the Undersheriff Randal Hicken," Immanuel said.

The mayor looked around and said nothing for a moment, then he got off his horse and handed the reins to one of his security men. He walked up real close to Uzziah and Immanuel in a conspiratorial manner.

"Look, fellas, if this is some kinda joke, it ain't funny," the mayor said.

"Well, there's this dodger out on us for $1000 fer that murder," Uzziah informed him.

"Listen, Randal Hicken was a disgrace to the city of St. Louis. The so-called sheriff's department that he was a member of was a part of that disgrace. Nobody appointed those men, they might as well have been a bunch of vigilantes, and as a matter of fact, they were. We're getting ready to start a real police department under my administration. Besides, nobody, no prosecutor or judge is gonna wanna try ya fer the disappearance of some mangy, blood-thirsty vigilante. And this part is just between you, me, and them Injuns, I don't even care ifn ya did disappear Hicken, he deserved it. Besides, we got bigger fish to fry, and the reward offered fer them was $5,000!" he said and raised both his eyebrows twice, a sure sign that he sure did have bigger fish. The mustache looked lonely when the eyebrows went away and happier when they returned to their original position.

"Who done what?" Immanuel asked.

"Where ya been, in the sticks?" the sheriff asked.

"Well, yeah, that's exactly where we been," Uzziah said.

"Figures, four darkies broke into a bank, but was discovered by two bank tellers returning from dinner, those poor boys should have been home and in bed. Them blacks kilt the two White bank tellers, stole the money, then set the bank on fire to hide their crimes."

"No kiddin'?" Immanuel said, amused that their murder of Hicken had boiled down to nothing but a public service.

"We's gonna hang 'em high, day after tommarie," Daggett said, and wiped his forefinger back and forth under his squirrel and so they could both see him smile.

"Where's the hangin' gonna be?" Uzziah asked.

"Duncan's Island, but hell, we already sold near 20,000 tickets at a buck and a half a piece to have everybody steam paddled out there to watch the ceremonies. There'll be hot dogs, and candy, games fer the kids, and a picnic before the hangings. But I don't think there's any way fer ya to get out there, since all the tickets are sold. Ifn I was you two, I'd take yer band of Injuns and get the hell out afore people start lookin' fer others to hang, ya know it can get to be a fever!" the mayor of St. Louis said, walked back, took the reins from his security man, and mounted up.

The group of men rode off, much to the surprise of the other White men and the Crow.

"What's going on, son?" Patrick asked Immanuel, and Immanuel kept noticing that Patrick relished calling him *son*.

"Well, we're yesterday's news it seems, let's get these Crows outta chere and across the Mississippi and Uzziah and I will explain everythin'," Immanuel said.

They mounted up and rode the ten or so blocks to the Mississippi River. There was an island which lay halfway between Illinois and Missouri, and they swam their horses to it by going way upstream and riding the current down to it.

It was heavily wooded, and they decided to make camp there that night and get back on the trail to the Rockies the next day.

While they were making camp, Buffalo Warrior walked up to Uzziah and Immanuel.

"We will continue back to our sacred lands tonight," he said in Crow

"Aint' ya hungry?" Uzziah asked in Crow.

"Yes, we are hungry for the plains and the mountains, we have seen enough of the way the White man lives. This journey will be recounted many times, but I still don't know why we did it." Buffalo Warrior said. Standing Bear was nearby, and she took him aside and said goodbye, and Immanuel could hear her trying to explain why nothing had happened.

Finally, after Buffalo Warrior had listened for a while, he said, "I understand, they go for deer, but had already captured bear."

That was as good an explanation as any.

As Uzziah cooked the meal for the nine men, himself included, he watched with a sort of nostalgia as the Crow braves rode off toward the west.

"That was an amazing thing they did for us," he said to Immanuel, who was standing there sipping on the bottle of whiskey he'd taken from Uzziah's saddlebags.

"Hey, is that my bottle?" Uzziah asked.

"Yeah, yer the onliest one who ever has one," Immanuel said, smiling.

———

After they had eaten and everyone had turned in, Immanuel kept hearing voices coming from the other end of the island. The wind was carrying them to their campsite.

"Ya hear that?" he asked Uzziah.

"Yeah, somebody else must be on the island," Uzziah said.

They mounted up after everyone else had gone to their bedrolls and rode toward the other edge of the island.

Coming from the dense copse of trees, they saw the gallows and the four nooses swaying in the wind. Vendors and merchants were the ones talking, they were setting up their booths where they would sell their wares the next day.

"What the hell?" Uzziah said.

"Brother, take away two nooses and that coulda been us, amusement for the masses, so to speak," Immanuel whispered, and they turned their horses, Trevor and Shadow, and traveled back to their camp.

They didn't have any trouble waking up in the morning, the falderal which was wafting down from the other end of the island was getting louder and louder as some of the 20,000 who had bought tickets were arriving to watch the hangings. They decided that they would ride down into the woods where they'd spied the gallows and watch before they rode back west. Later, they would decide that that had been a bad decision.

———

Even though July 9th, 1841, was a Friday, the town of St. Louis had decided to treat it as a holiday. The hangings would take place in the afternoon on Dunkin's Island, and the city had made $30,000 from the sale of the tickets, and that didn't even count the percentage which the mayor would get from those he had allowed on the island as merchants and sellers of paraphernalia.

Mayor Daggett was leaving his office in the court-house when he was approached by a good-looking woman who looked like she was all business. There was a man with her whose head was on a swivel and looked like a bodyguard.

"Mayor Daggett," the woman said.

"Yes, I'm Mayor Daggett, how can I be of assistance?" he said. The man was always looking for votes.

"I'm Pinkerton Agent Kate Warnes, and this is my assistant, Tom Branch." He still hadn't shown much improvement on the firing range, but his antics in her boudoir had gotten much better. Besides, every woman deserved arm candy, and Tom, the not-so-good-shot Pinkerton Agent, was just that.

Mayor Daggett shook hands with Tom, while Kate had offered her hand first.

"Sorry, still can't get used to women shaking hands," Daggett said, and he took her hand and tried to kiss it as she jerked it away.

"I understand that a raid of Crow Indians came riding into St. Louis yesterday and that among that rabble there were two White men named Immanuel James Jones and Uzziah Ferguson O'Bannon." She seemed anxious when she mentioned those names, and he wondered why.

"I never got their last names, but their Christian names were as you mentioned," Daggett said.

"Are they in your jail?"

"No, why would they be?"

"There was a $1,000 reward apiece on those two for the murder of one of your undersheriffs," she said. "Where did you put them?"

"I told them what I knew and let them go," Mayor Daggett said.

"What!?!"

At that *what* Tom pulled his concealed weapon from his shoulder holster and was pointing up and down the hallway.

"Put that away, Tom, or you'll hurt somebody," Kate Warne commanded him. Reluctantly, he reholstered his weapon.

"Where are they now?" Warne asked.

"Probably at the hangin'," Daggett said. "I have a private boat, would ya like to accompany me?"

———

Twenty minutes later, Daggett, Tom, and Kate Warne were aboard his private vessel and making their way to Duncan's Island.

"My God, there must be half of St. Louis out here," Warne commented.

"More like three-quarters, we done sold 20,000 tickets, the paddle wheelers are still bringing the rest of the crowd over from the docks."

———

Uzziah, Immanuel, Patrick—Immanuel's pa—and Sean —Uzziah's pa—and Uzziah's two brothers, Raymond and Hank, were all mingling with the crowd at the hanging. Hank had bought his ma, Rahab, a nice silk scarf for what he said would have cost him twice as much in Virginia. Raymond was looking for something for his girlfriend, and Uzziah was teasing him endlessly about having such a thing.

"Maybe mountain men don't like women," Raymond retorted.

"Oh, we like 'em all right, we just wish they'd turn into jerked meat once ya screwed 'em," Immanuel said, and both Hank and Raymond were bent over in laughter at that remark.

"Son, that wasn't a very pleasant remark," Patrick scolded Immanuel.

"Pleasant or not, ya tell me what do ya do with a woman after ya shot yer wad?"

"Hold her," Patrick suggested, at which Immanuel and Uzziah both laughed.

"And that right there, Pa, is why yer married, and I'm not!" Immanuel said.

———

Kate Warne and Tom Branch were perusing the crowd in hopes of finding the two men who had traveled from Chicago. The reward on the dodgers hadn't been enough, but who would have guessed such an astronomical amount for four Black men!?!

The crowd milling about had settled down as the time for the hangings drew near. That was a help, less milling and more settled would leave the two men she wanted easier to see.

She knew that Tom knew what both men looked like, and possibly with both sets of their eyes, they could catch them. She had brought along a pair of binoculars and was scanning the now quieted crowd as conversations stopped as the four negroes were marched up on the gallows. Of course, Mayor Daggett wasn't going to miss an opportunity for him to gather votes, so after the condemned men were situated in front of their drop slots and the nooses were put around their necks, Daggett stepped to the front of the gallows for a political moment.

"Ladies and gentlemen," he began, and his voice rang out like any true orator, and the crowd was stilled and quiet. "Today, we are gathered on what some have always referred to as Bloody Island, and as you probably know, it was called that because of the illicit duels which were fought here in days gone by. But today, Bloody Island takes on a new meaning for two young, good-looking tellers from one of our banks who were murdered by this foursome, then if that weren't enough, their stripped and mutilated bodies were burned in the hopes of covering up these vicious and ungodly acts." He paused there as the crowd got into it, by hissing and booing the four who were about to meet their deaths. Daggett held up his hands for silence, but he loved it!

"As the trapdoors are tripped, these four young and dangerous men will take a trip to hell!" Again, he paused as the crowd cheered and applauded. "But this city, this great city, the gateway to the west, St. Louis, will be a safer place tonight. When we tuck in our sons and daughters this evening, they will have seen the consequences of murderous acts, and four less bad men will roam the city. But please know, if I am reelected mayor of this great metropolitan city, I will create a complete and newly armed police force, which shall roam the city, not to violate the law, but to uphold it!" He paused and was disappointed in the lackluster response he had gotten for his campaign promise. Well, if the crowd wanted blood, then it was blood he would give them.

"And now, what you have all come for," he said and he gestured toward the gallows where a man dressed all in black walked toward the trip handle which would release the doors on all four murderers.

You could have heard a pin drop, and while this moment of luxurious silence held the crowd in suspense, Kate Warne decided to do something unusual.

"Immanuel & Uzziah!!" she screamed at the top of her voice, and to her eyes she had the binocs. There were only two heads which turned from the suspense of the drops, and as she had guessed, it was her wanted duo.

In the next half second, there came a mutual gasp from the 20,000 gathered there as four men dropped and you could hear the snapping of their necks.

"Come on!" Immanuel said to Uzziah as he grabbed his partner and pushed him through the now docile crowd. There was only one way to get to their horses from there, straight under the gallows. Uzziah shrank back in hopes of not hitting the legs of any of the condemned, but did so anyway.

"STOP THOSE MURDERERS!" Tom yelled on cue per Kate Warne's orders, and 20,000 people surged forward at the gallows and running under them just as the aforementioned murderers had done, the bodies of the newly executed Black men swinging back and forth from the rush and contact of the crowd—it was simple mathematics, the crowd reached Uzziah and Immanuel before they could reach their horses and they began to tear them apart when pistols shots rang into the after-noon air.

"Those are my prisoners!" Kate Warne yelled and, swinging her pistol back and forth, cleared the crowd in front of her, and Tom did something right, he stepped forward and put the cuffs on Uzziah and Immanuel as the crowd cheered.

8

Nobody knew what exactly had happened, except Immanuel and Uzziah. The minute they were in cuffs and put on the mayor's private boat and taken back to St. Louis, they realized two things. St. Louis could have cared less about the disappearance of Randal Hicken, and the reward had obviously been put up by Allen Pinkerton of the Pinkerton Agency.

Kate Warne had come down to St. Louis on a private train which was owned by the Agency, and now, she was taking no chances. She had had Uzziah in cuffs before, and his miraculous escape from the paddle wheeler when Immanuel, whom they thought had been drowned, rescued his partner, well, nothing like that was going to happen again, ever again!

They put the two suspects in a carriage and took them to the train station, where they put them in irons in the special jail car which Allan Pinkerton had had built. There were slots in the door for food and water to be passed through, and a hole in the floor just big enough to crap and pee through, and that was it. They were going to stay locked in that special car till it reached Chicago, and then they would be arraigned for the murder of Pinkerton Agent Robert Spells.

The following night, after the prisoners had been taken to their special cells, Allen Pinkerton and Kate Warne sat in a downtown Chicago restaurant, and he ordered them both steaks. He was beaming. His investment in the first female detective had finally, and forever, paid off. He had paid quite a bit of money for her to chase the supposed murderers of one of her fellow agents, one Robert Spells. Robert had convinced the Agency to let him go after the killers of an undersheriff from St. Louis. As it had turned out, that murder would never be solved because, like so many in law enforcement, the fine line between what they did and what criminals did was too often blurred by circumstances. Hadn't Allan Pinkerton himself fled Scotland because he was involved in insurrectionary activities which had resulted in a warrant for his arrest?

And it seemed that Undersheriff Randal Hicken had been misusing his powers and acting from what was essentially a mercenary vigilante organization. A lot of people thought some law, any law, was better than no law at all.

The mayor of St. Louis had not even bothered to arrest the two mountain men when they turned themselves in for the crime. They hadn't admitted it, but the high...well, Pinkerton thought it was high when he put the bounty on their head's dead or alive, but as it would happen, a more heinous murder case had gripped St. Louis, and the four negroes responsible had swung out from the gallows and paid for their crimes. But, brilliant, brilliant Kate Warne had gone to the hangings and, following her impeccable instincts, had found those two mountain men enjoying the hangings, and that was exactly where she had arrested them.

Now, they were locked in the agency's jail in downtown Chicago, awaiting trial for the murder of one of their young agents.

Allan Pinkerton knew the circuit judge of the 7th Judicial Court, which served about five counties, and Cook County was among them. Pinkerton had donated a lot of money to that particular judge's campaign. He owed Pinkerton, and that debt was sure to be paid when the trail got underway.

Yes, there was nothing but circumstantial evidence against the men, but the mountain of circumstances did nothing if not point to Uzziah Ferguson O'Bannon and Immanuel James Jones as the two mountain men who should be held responsible for the death of the young and eager Pinkerton Agent.

The steaks arrived and they were cooked perfectly to Pinkerton's arrangement—medium rare—with a pool of blood surrounding the bottom of the steaks and bumping up against the mashed garlic potatoes that this place did so well. A loaf of fresh hot bread was placed upon the table, and Allen bowed his head and held out his hand to Kate.

She took his hand, even though she was more of a modern woman than he would have suspected, and in her heart of hearts, doubted the possibility of a God in heaven watching over us all and allowing all the evil that was happening.

"Father," Pinkerton began, "we give thanks not only

for this meal, but for the energies and talents of this brilliant woman sitting with me at this table. I pray that you will bless us with a conviction on those two trashy men who live like savages and act thusly, too. We remember Robert Spells and his enthusiasm as he headed out of Chicago for the wasteland of the Rocky Mountains. Bring us a guilty verdict and let us have these two brutes swinging out over eternity as we bring them to justice."

———

Both Uzziah and Immanuel were totally beat by the time they made it to the Pinkerton Agency's private jail. It was well accommodated and had all the latest in materials. There were no windows, and there was a three-foot floor made of poured concrete. The bars were steel, and the ceiling was another poured from above floor of three feet of concrete. It was nothing if not impregnable.

"Ya notice how the sound don't travel inside this cell?" Uzziah asked Immanuel. They were separated into two cells by steel bars like the ones that surrounded them.

"At least it's clean," Immanuel said.

"Oh yeah, like things being clean ever matter to ya!"

"I am a clean individual," Immanuel protested.

"Yeah, how 'bout that time I had to throw ya in the river 'cause ya was scaring all the game away?"

"Now, a man can lose track of the last time his body had been baptized by the waters of cleanliness."

"Ya got a nose, don't ya?" Uzziah protested.

"Uh-huh, and somethin' smells fishy 'bout how she found us at that hangin'," Immanuel complained.

"I told ya we shouldn't stick 'round to see those poor bastards drop," Uzziah said, putting his head in his hands.

"Like hell."

"I did. I said why would we want to see someone swing when we was faced with the same possibility. Did I not say that?"

"Ya did, I'll have to admit it," Immanuel said.

"So, ifn we had left when I suggested, left with the Crows who brung us, then yer admitting that we wouldn't be sittin' here about to go on trial for a young man's stupidity?" Uzziah asked.

"If only he'd completely lost his memory," Immanuel moaned.

"If only, if only, if only," Uzziah said, then added, "If only we'd have taken away his stuff when we found him froze to death, they wouldn't have recovered that notebook with perfect pictures drawn by the dead man, well, they wasn't drawn by a dead man, ya understand, but drawn before he died, and what about all those notes he made, evidently this is how they hope to see us punished for his freezing to death."

"Punishment is one thing, but did ya see those four poor bastards we had to run through as they was hangin' there?"

"Yeah, I saw 'em, I smelled 'em, and I touched a couple as I ran by," Uzziah said.

"What'd ya do that fer? That's probably the reason they caught us, don't ever touch a dying man, which reminds me this all started when ya helped Benjamin die."

"He was strangling—"

"And he and his partner Roscoe tried to blow us into smithereens!" Immanuel reminded Uzziah.

"I could not let him strangle like that."

"I'm sure he appreciated it, he'll probably send ya a thank you note from hell, or, ifn we get our butts convicted, ya can get thanked in person when we end up there!" Immanuel was on a tare. He had been caught, and he wanted a drink and if he couldn't have that, well, he wanted to point a finger!

"I am not goin' to hell," Uzziah said, standing up and looking at Immanuel.

"You ain't?"

"Nope."

"How can ya say that after all the shite we done?"

"Easy, I got a Savior who took human form, and being found in human likeness, he humbled himself to the point of death, even death on a cross."

"Will ya cut out that quotin' scripture, will ya, please."

"It's the livin' and breathin' word of God!" Uzziah shouted.

"No, it ain't—it's just an ancient book that peoples kept translatin' and printin' and probably the whole world would be a lot better off ifn they had lost the damned thing!"

By this time, both men were standing at the bars which separated each of their cells, and staring at each other.

"Don't ever say that about the Bible again, partner," Uzziah almost pleaded.

"I ain't yer partner."

"Oh, no, well, what the hell are we doin' here together?"

"It's like a lot of my life, a pure dee mistake, yer just a hillbilly from Virginia that shared a whore with me, and ya bamboozled yer way into my life, that's it! That's all of it!" Immanuel said as he curled up on his cot and pulled the meager blanket over him.

Uzziah stood there and looked at Immanuel's back. There was the man who had basically turned him into the man that he was today, and everything Immanuel had just said was simply not true. Hadn't his partner said time and again, how glad he was that they had met up, or were those just the times when Uzziah had a jug in his saddlebag? He had misused his influence over the man by always having a jug for him, it wasn't right, and if they got out of this, he was not going to continue to do that, he wasn't.

God, he wanted to say something that would make his partner Immanuel take back those hurtful words, both about himself and about the Father who created us all. Immanuel had to realize, the only way they were going to get out of these troubles, these circumstances, was to rely on the grace and protection of the Father— that's all there was to it!

———

The trial date was set for early in September, right before the fall weather set in. Patrick Gass had sent letters to Edgar Allan Poe and asked if he and his wife Ginny could make the trip to Chicago for the trial. Patrick thought that it was important that Edgar and his son Monty met so that Monty could be introduced to this new way of thinking—ratiocination.

Poe wrote back that he would travel there as long as his expenses and those of his wife Ginny were reimbursed. Patrick wrote back and stated unequivocally that their expenses would be covered and also mentioned the fine hotels in Chicago where he hoped Poe would stay. It was the same hotel that Gass, his son Monty, Sean O'Bannon, and his two sons were staying in, and it seemed Gass was fronting the bill on all of them. This was a financial burden for Patrick Gass, but one he was not only willing to take, but glad to assume, since he had just met his eldest son from the Mandan woman and hoped that he would not be hung in his presence.

The Gass family had many friends, among them the only surviving leader of the Lewis and Clark Expedition, Merriweather Lewis. He and Gass had become great friends after the expedition, and Clark had introduced him to Jefferson and his eldest daughter, Martha Jefferson—later Martha Jefferson Randolph. It wasn't that the Patrick Gass family became famous as much as they moved within prominent circles in Washington, and their eldest son, Montague, after becoming a lawyer, moved easily within circles of the well-known elite in Washington.

Needless to say, none of this was lost on the society of Chicago and the Grand Wolverine Hotel, which gave their esteemed guests rates that were not the norm, but just having such people stay there meant so much.

When all who were going to preside for the defense of Immanuel and Uzziah were gathered together at the hotel dining room, lunch was served, and afterward, war plans were made.

"I am so appreciative that all of you who are gathered here at this luncheon are willing to testify at the—I think—absurd trial of these two mountain men. Of course, the most prestigious of our guests at this table is Captain William Clark." There was a rapping on the table, which was the same as applause in those days.

"I'm not sure what my great, good friend, Patrick Gass, expects of me here. I do not know the men in question, and am not sure what I will bring to their defense," Clark quite frankly said.

"What you bring," Patrick said, "is the knowledge that deep into the Louisiana territory there was, and still is, a sense of law which does not contradict the rule of law established in these eastern states, but supplants it when there are no authorities to dictate what is and is not proper."

"If you're referring to the sense of busking it, like we did as we were on the trail. I do know that the majority of those who have inhabited the hills and heights of the Rockies have enabled this county to defeat the French, the British, and the Spanish when it came to the control of those hills and heights. And for that reason, if no other, I am happy to be here."

"Can you tell us anything you gained by interviewing the suspects in this trial?" Monty Gass asked.

"Yes, yes, I can. Actually, Mr. Poe accompanied me on this visit to the fortified Pinkerton jailhouse, and I must say, it's a good thing we're not here trying to break them out of there!" Clark said. That got a good laugh, though Patrick and Sean had already discussed what would happen if they were convicted and what lengths they might go to liberate them from custody. However, the best bet was to free them legally, then they would no longer have to face any more troubles concerning these charges.

"Edgar, I do hope you don't mind if I call you that?" Monty asked.

"Not at all," Poe said and removed his hand from that of his wife, who had accompanied him to the luncheon, much to the surprise of the others.

"What were your impressions of my half brother Immanuel and his partner Uzziah?"

"I'm actually glad you asked me that. These men are not a throwback to an earlier type of man who might, or might not, have existed on the earth. I enjoyed their banter, their arguing was most humorous, and their ability to take the jib, and give it, was hearty. They told me and Mr. Clark the entire story, and it varied in many ways from the published article that circulated in many papers written by one Austin Fielder. In fact, we were told many more details about their relationship with Roger Spells, the Pinkerton Agent, and even though Agent Spells was determined to arrest them for a crime which the city of St. Louis has decided now is not a crime at all, they gave the Agent every opportunity to leave them alone.

"So, here we have a great example of men improvising what they thought to be a justice, albeit a justice of the frontier, and showing a great deal of mercy in the implementation of that justice."

———

"What ya readin'?" Immanuel asked.

"That book that Mr. Poe brought," Uzziah said, not taking his eyes off the page.

"Boy, what a dandy, he wouldn't last five minutes in the mountains," Immanuel joked, but Uzziah simply turned his head and gave a stare to his partner.

"Are ya making some kinda separate deal with the prosecution, or what?"

Uzziah kept the book in his hand and sat up on his bunk. "Separate deal, what are ya takin' 'bout?"

"Well, I weren't the one who shot Agent Spells and got 'em all outta his head," Immanuel reminded Uzziah.

"Yeah, yeah, I done it, and am proud of it. It was a terrific shot at that range, and he didn't die, did he?"

"Nah, that's a fact."

"That deserter—what was his name?"

"His wife's name was Sally Anne," Immanuel said dreamily.

"Leave it to ya to 'member the good-lookin' young wife with the big tatas," Uzziah said.

Immanuel sat up on his bunk and gave Uzziah one of his looks. "Whose 'memberin' what?"

Uzziah blushed.

"Yer blushin', oh my God, we are facin' the gallows and yer blusin' 'bout 'memberin' her fabulous tits. Well, she did have 'em that's a fer sure, and, young son, ya have gotta get yer nose outta that Bible of yourn and into some pussy! Lead the life of a man, for God's sake!" Immanuel almost shouted.

"Real men read the Bible!" Uzziah shouted back.

"And real men 'member fabulous tatas. It's okay, young son, good tatas are great to 'member, they are."

"What the hell was we talkin' 'bout?" Uzziah asked.

"You asked me the name of the deserter, and it was

Clement Shaw. Then, I asked if ya was makin' a separate deal with the people that wanna stretch our necks," Immanuel reminded him, then added, "Ain't no separate nothin'—we live together, we die together, that's the way I sees it."

"Well, ya know back last week when they took me out fer an hour?" Uzziah asked.

"Was it that long? I awoke from a nap and ya was gone."

"They told me, the prosecutor told me, if I said ya done it and it was yern idea, that they'd swing ya, and I only get some prison time," Uzziah admitted.

"They did, huh?" Immanuel said, smiling like a fox, then said, "What'd ya tell 'em?"

"I said, sure, I'd take that deal in a second," Uzziah said with a straight face.

Immanuel stood up and walked to the bars that separated their cells, grabbed the bars, and looked at Uzziah. "Yer shittin' me, right?"

"Nah, I figured it was yer idea and most of it ya did, so why should I hang fer it," Uzziah said, looking down at his hands. "Besides, I ain't old like ya, got lots of years left to enjoy."

"Young son," Immanuel said, and now he was sounding serious, "this ain't a good time to pull my veritable leg, so, ifn yer tellin' the truth about being a traitor, ya got to tell me true."

"I'm sorry, old son, but it's the truth," Uzziah said, and Immanuel went back and sat on his bunk, the absolute picture of dejection.

"Ya swears on a Bible that ya told 'em that?" Immanuel said, looking at the floor.

"Can't do that, but I do swear this is the best I ever got that goat of yourn," Uzziah said, smiling.

"Ya son of a bitch!" Immanuel screamed, going to the bars again.

"Do not call my ma, Rahab, a bitch, old son."

"Forgive me, I almost lost my water, young son, I really did," Immanuel admitted.

"It kinda reminded me of when we was tellin' Spells who he was, lyin', lyin', lyin' right to the man's face."

"But he'd been shot in the head, what excuse do I have, ya damned sure learned how to lie like a mountain man, I can tell ya that," Immanuel said, smiling. "Come here, so I can break yer neck."

Uzziah walked to the bars and the two men grabbed each other through them.

"I'm glad we're friends, and I'm glad no matter what happens, it happens to both of us," Uzziah said.

Immanuel let go of Uzziah and quickly changed the subject.

"Okay." Immanuel laughed. "But old Spells sure as hell lost every memory he'd ever had."

"And Rose Water popped his cherry," Uzziah said, remembering.

"Yers, too if I 'member right, well, as far as Injun pussy went that is," Immanuel added.

"Don't suppose he knew he was gonna be workin' fer ole Jedediah Younger, did he?" Uzziah reminisced, knowing that neither of them wanted to dwell on the possibility of the upcoming hangings.

"Younger worked that poor boy like a mule, and took Rose Water with 'em," Immanuel said.

"At least we got Charlie out of the deal." Leave it to Uzziah to remember the boy who had been born to Rose, the baby they'd taken to the settlement where Ophelia, now Standing Bear, raised him up like one of his own.

"Young son, ifn we do swing, the trip will have been worth it," Immanuel said, looking with his thousand-yard stare back toward the past that he and his partner had enjoyed. Uzziah almost teared up thinking that they'd have no more times together to argue, drink, and share women.

9

When Uzziah Ferguson O'Bannon and Immanuel James Jones entered the courtroom, it was the first time they had been out of that cage of the Pinkerton Agency since their arrest during the quadruple hangings on Blood Island opposite St. Louis, Missouri. They had been given a bucket of cold water and a bar of soap each and told they would have to wear their deerskins into the trial. That was fine by them.

When they were taken from the Agency lockup to the Federal Courthouse in downtown Chicago, they were hustled into a black box of a wagon and driven. When they got out, both mountain men looked up at the September firmament, which was bright blue with scattered cumulus clouds scudding across the morning sky. Neither of them could take their eyes off that beautiful sight. They were mountain men and had lived in the wild and never had their senses been denied the aromas and sights of nature. Officers pushed them toward the back door of the courthouse, and both of them were screaming at the top of their lungs right into each other's faces.

"WAGH!!" they both screamed, the phlegm from their yelling being thrown into the other's face, but they couldn't have cared less, they were—for this moment— free men, and free men express themselves into their freedom.

Disgusted, the guards dragged them into the courthouse, and the smiles on their faces did not disappear even as they were led into the courtroom, where twelve men sat in the jury box, and the tables for the defense and the prosecution sat opposite each other, and the trial was about to begin.

Beside the jury of twelve men, good and true, sat the prosecution's table with two men in suits seated behind it, and away from the jury in front of the judge was the table for the defense. At that particular table, Immanuel recognized his half brother Monty Gass and the poet/writer Edgar Allan Poe, who had brought the book to their cells and interviewed them. So, a poet and a lawyer, that seemed about right to both the mountain men.

Immanuel and Uzziah looked at the men who were going to sit in judgment on them, the men who would say whether they were innocent or guilty, the men who would say whether they would swing or be set free.

They were seated at the table for the defense, just down from Edgar Allan Poe and Montague Gass. Monty leaned across Poe and whispered to them.

"It's very important that you don't say anything unless asked to by the court, do you both understand?"

Both of them nodded that they did.

"All rise!" the bailiff announced, and everyone in

the courtroom stood. "The Honorable Judge Theophilus W. Smith now presiding in the 7th Judicial Court of the County of Cook and the state of Illinois."

Judge Smith sat down. "You may be seated," the bailiff said, and everyone sat back down.

"Will the defendants please rise," Judge Smith said, and Immanuel and Uzziah stood, and so did Monty Gass.

"You men have been charged with the unlawful and premeditated death of Robert Q. Spells while he was acting as an Agent for the Pinkerton Detective Agency. How do you plead?"

"On my knees," Immanuel said quite seriously, and the gallery—at least some of them—guffawed.

"My clients plead not guilty, Your Honor," Monty spoke up, trying to cover Immanuel's answer.

Judge Smith looked long and hard at Immanuel. "You are too old to be impertinent by mistake. I will not tolerate your sarcasm, jokes, jibs, jests, witticisms, quips, old chestnuts, gags, wisecracks, or any other form of answering which would elicit a response from the gallery. Do you understand, Immanuel James Jones?"

"Yes," Immanuel said.

"Yes, what?"

Monty whispered into Immanuel's ear.

"Yes, Your Honor."

"The prosecution will make their opening statement," the judge said.

Monty signaled for Immanuel and Uzziah to be seated.

A man stood up. He was maybe forty years old. He wore a longish black coat, which to both Immanuel and Uzziah had the unfortunate look of an undertaker. The jacket had a velvet black collar which ran down half the lapel, the other portion was the same material as the jacket. His tie was black, and it was wrapped around his neck at the collar line with the collar sticking up out of the tie and framing his chin and face. His shirtsleeves showed, barely at the end of the coat sleeves, and the trousers were a slightly different color black, and broke nicely over a highly polished pair of black boots, the height of which was impossible to guess. He strode before the table of defense and raised a white handkerchief to his nose upon smelling the two men seated there. He turned abruptly, almost as if he were executing a military about-face, and turned back toward the jurors, and as he arrived before them, he put the handkerchief away since they smelled like him—all soap and cologne.

"Gentlemen of the jury." The words washed over the jurors who sat taller, having been knighted with the title of *gentlemen* by one, and he looked intently at them as if he weren't sure what his next words would be, but he was, oh yes, he was sure.

"This case is unusual for two very distinct reasons. First of all, a man from our ranks, a gentleman like us, employed by the distinguished Pinkerton Agency, was assigned the job of finding those two men!" At *those two men*, he turned again with military precision and pointed at Immanuel and Uzziah! And the manner in which he said, *those two men* was delivered in a lower register as if to suggest that they were lower than gentlemen.

"Robert Spells found those two men, oh yes, he did, and what happened to Agent Robert Spells after that is not a mystery. Why? You might ask, very simply, it was because, as Robert's mother will later testify, Robert had kept a journal since the age of ten, and now, in his mid-twenties, his journal taking was quite factual and explicit. Robert Spells was also an accomplished student of drawing, and when he made his nightly notes in his journal, he was able, through excellent and prodigious memory, to recreate the very image of the people he talked to. Some are beginning to call that sort of memory photographic, but suffice it to say, once he saw you, he did not forget your face or what you had done in his company.

"The prosecution will establish that not only did Agent Robert Spells find those two accused men, but he was assaulted by them, the scar at his left temple once his body was found testifying to that effect, and if that weren't enough, he wrote about being shot by one of them early in his investigation. That scar along the side of his head is Robert's testimony that they did try to kill him.

"If that were not enough, after being shot and losing the memory of himself, he was placed into servitude to another wild mountain man by the name of Jedidiah Younger who then worked like a slave the poor amnesiac to the point of death, and having been a man of loose morals, Mr. Younger introduced Agent Spells, whom he called Toby, who thought his name was simply Toby with no last name, and introduced the poor boy into the world of whores and whoring. Robert worked for pennies, then spent those very pennies on the Indian whore who slept with any and all men who gave her fifty cents.

"When his memory returned one afternoon during his drudgery for Jedidiah Younger, he tried to escape and was chased and forced to pull Jedidiah from his horse, and by using Jedidiah's pistol, forced the older mountain man to tell him his true identity. He was clubbed by Jedidiah, then tied to a tree and was slathered with bacon grease and left for the varmints to eat him.

"When a mountain cougar and a grizzly bear showed up to finish Robert off, it was only by the grace of God that those two ferocious animals fought each other for the prize of eating Robert Spells, and in the ferocious fight, the grizzly winning. During this battle which was, if you will, a great example of what both predators could and would do to him, Robert was able to release himself from the ropes, and ran from the grizzly into the cabin of Jedidiah, where he lit a stick of dynamite and, throwing the lit stick into the box of six other sticks, ran from the cabin directly before it exploded.

"I'm almost through. After losing his memory, being worked like a white salve, and forced to copulate with natives, Robert Spells, remembering his identity, escaped, but being from Chicago got lost, where he was discovered by the two mountain men sitting at the defense table, Immanuel James Jones and Uzziah Ferguson O'Bannon. Immanuel shot Robert in the hand for trying to discipline his horse, and he was taken back to their cabins.

"And here, gentlemen of the jury, is the heinous part of these two mountain men's crimes against the Pinkerton Agent Robert Spells. After the winter snows had fallen and knowing that he could not find his way from the mountains, they blind folded him and took him to a desolate place and left him to freeze to death.

He was discovered where he was left by Pinkerton Agent Kate Warne, and his prodigious journals, notes, and drawings were found with him. They had to be pried from his frozen hands.

"And the defense will try to tell you that they did not kill Robert Spells, but what do you call grazing a man with a high-powered rifle, selling him into slavery to another mountain man, then finding him lost after breaking away from that slave master, then waiting till the snow was four foot deep and dropping him off in the middle of nowhere to find his way back to civilization. Gentlemen of the jury, we, the state of Illinois, will prove beyond a shadow of a doubt that this was done, all of it with malicious intent, with the only possible outcome being the death of Pinkerton Agent Robert Spells."

The prosecutor sat down beside his assistant.

"Thank you, Mr. Rawlings, and now, Mr...." He had to look at the notes on his desk. "Yes, of course, Mr. Gass," he said and smiled as if he'd made a joke. Some of the gallery got the joke and giggled. Judge Smith frowned at those who had had the nerve to snicker in his courtroom.

Monty Gass stood, he was taller than Mr. Rawlings by an inch or two, and Immanuel thought if this was a contest concerning who could beat whose ass, his bet was on Gass.

Monty was dressed well for the Baltimore courts. He was in the traditional black, but instead of wearing black trousers, they were a cream color, and his tie was the same color and was tied in a rather big bow beneath his chin. His coat was a waistcoat with tails, and it was cut to show the dark brown speckled vest that fit him to a tee. The tails stopped about three inches above the back of his knees, and his shoes had a square bootcut toe and were tied.

He walked away from the jury so that the whole gallery could see him, and he could see everyone in the courtroom.

"Gentlemen of the jury, today we come before the court with a most unusual case. It resembles no case that I have read and, in doing so, takes its place among things that you, the gentlemen of the jury, might be guilty of. I know in Baltimore, there is a rather substantial group of people who can only be considered homeless. Why, last winter, I looked out and saw a man wrapped up in blankets across the street from my townhouse. He had a woolen hat pulled down over his head, a large beard, and substantial boots. I'd seen him before out there, when the weather was mercilessly cold. He slept on the street. Now, I could have invited him into my townhouse, but that is not the practice of those of us in the city. We can't know why he's out there, what crimes he may or may not have committed, all we know is, he's sleeping on the freezing streets—"

"I object, Your Honor, what can this hypothetical possibly have to do with the case at hand?!?" Mr. Rawlings was standing and expecting a ruling from the court.

"Overruled, Mr. Rawlings, and I, for one, am insulted by such egregious behavior." The judge ruled and his gavel went down. "Any more objections when they are not necessary may be, and most certainly will be, overruled if you continue with this," Judge Smith said.

"Sorry, Your Honor," Rawlings said and sat down like a scolded schoolboy.

Monty Gass knew that Rawlings's objection had nothing to do with the law and everything to do with interrupting Monty's story.

"I'll forget about that particular man lying on the freezing street, and go to another example. One given to me by my law professor at Yale. You've just won a million dollars in cash. There is one stipulation, you must collect it before sundown. Your notice of the winning was given to you an hour before sundown, and you must leave your house, cross a rather long bridge, underneath which flows a roaring river, and walk another half a mile to the lottery office, where you will collect your money.

"While crossing the bridge, there stands a man with a long rope wrapped tightly around his waist. He throws the other end of the rope to you and says, 'Save me!' right before he jumps off the bridge. Tell me, gentlemen of the jury, would you save such a deranged person or simply drop the rope and continue on to your destination to collect your million dollars?"

Uzziah looked at the jurors, he was interested in such hypotheticals of morality, and he could see the faces of the twelve men going through the machinations of good men, and also thinking of all that money.

"Obviously, you don't need to answer that," Monty continued after giving the time to ruminate, "but the legal question would be, would you be responsible for that deranged man's death if you walked on? And further, even if you felt guilty for not helping him, is that the same as murder?

"The legal definition of murder is, ***the unlawful killing of a human being with malice afore-thought.*** Did you walk onto that bridge with malice against the man? Were your actions on the bridge premeditated and deliberate? Well, you did deliberately throw the rope down, but does this constitute murder?

"It does not, gentlemen of the jury, any more than my clients up in the Rocky Mountains who had no malice aforethought when they left Mr. Robert Spellings in the mountains, with food, a loaded gun, a knife, and a healthy horse. How could these actions, granting the man the ability to survive, constitute the unlawful killing of a human being—"

Rawlings was on his feet, and before he could speak, the judge just motioned for him to sit back down.

"Remember, there is a burden of proof which lies at the feet of the prosecution, they must pick that burden up and carry it to the end of the trial. If they do not, then this is nothing more than civilized people, namely Allan Pinkerton, and Kate Warne seeking a revenge through the courts, and that, gentlemen of the jury, is tantamount to the misuse of justice and, on the part of the aforementioned duo, may suggest misfeasance at the very least or perhaps even fall over into malfeasance, which is intentional conduct which is wrongful or unlawful. Thank you."

"I object, Your Honor," Rawlings said after jumping up.

"Continue," Judge Smith said.

"All these hypotheticals thrown around by Mr. Gass are doing nothing but blurring what will be presented by the prosecution," Rawlings said.

"I am just discussing the evidence I believe will be introduced," Monty said.

"Overruled," Judge Smith said.

Monty walked back to the defense table, and

Immanuel whispered to Uzziah, "Damn, that man has a vocabulary, don't he?"

"Mr. Rawlings, please call your first witness," Judge Smith ordered.

"I call Samantha Spells to the stand," he said as an older woman in her late forties came from the back of the courtroom. She walked with a certain attitude of defeat, which is not unusual for those in mourning. The bailiff walked up to her as she stood in front of the witness seat.

"Place your right hand on the Bible."

She did so.

"Do you swear to tell the truth, the whole truth, and nothing but the truth, so help you God?"

"I do."

"Please be seated."

Rawlings got up and walked over to the witness stand and stood formally before her.

"Will you state for the court your name and your relationship to the deceased?"

"I am Samantha Spells, the mother of Robert Spells."

"Thank you. Tell me—may I call you Samantha?"

"Certainly."

"Tell us, Samantha, how did you come to find out about the death of your son, Robert?"

"That lady right there—"

"The court will note that Samantha Spells is pointing to Pinkerton Agent Kate Warne."

"So noted," the stenographer said.

"And was Agent Warne alone?"

"No, Allan Pinkerton, the man sitting next to Kate, was with her."

"What did they tell you?"

"I was informed that my son, Robert Spells, we called him Robbie, was found dead in the Rocky Mountains."

"And were you surprised?"

"Well, yes, Robbie was working in Chicago, we thought, and then, all of a sudden, he wasn't working here, but out west, and dead, what was I supposed to think?"

"Have you seen Robert's notebooks after they were pried from his frozen hands?"

"Yes, he was always a good drawer, and he liked to write about how his life was going."

"Could you read the section I have underlined in your son's journal?" Rawlings asked and handed the leather journal to Samantha.

"Certainly," she said and cleared her throat. "*I found the two men who were wanted for the murder of the Undersheriff Randal Hicken—*"

"I object, Your Honor," Monty said, standing up.

"On what grounds, Mr. Gass?"

"There is no longer a warrant under issue for the murder of Randal Hicken."

"The stenographer will strike that last statement of Mrs. Spells," Judge Smith said, and she nodded and crossed the shorthand remarks out on her notebook.

"Please continue to read after that remark," Rawlings said.

"Certainly, *I found them, but it makes no difference. Immanuel shot me in the right hand and then took my weapons from me. I am essentially their prisoner and there's little hope of escape before the winter sets in.*"

"Thank you, Samantha, that's all I have for this witness, Your Honor."

"Would you care to cross-examine, Mr. Gass?" Judge Smith said.

"Yes, Your Honor, I would."

Monty Gass walked up near the witness stand, but did not get too close.

"I am sorry about the death of your young son. You have my deepest sympathies. It's painful for any of us when those younger than we are, and especially our children, die. Again, you have my condolences."

"Thank you."

"What was Robert like when he was a boy?"

"He was a boy, like all boys," she said.

"Yes, of course, but did he dream of going west and making his fortune, or being the hero in one of those dime novels that most children read?"

"No, he was a homebody," she said.

"I see, then did it surprise you when he became a Pinkerton Agent?"

"Well, he was a sort of glorified security guard, you know, going around shaking door handles and making sure places were locked up and secure."

"And you may not know this, but Allan Pinkerton has made it known through his hiring practices that he hires women, minorities—did you know this?"

"Well, I was a little taken aback when they hired Robbie, he wasn't exactly the outdoors type, and had never gone camping, shot a gun of any type, or even slept outside in the backyard like some boys liked to do."

"So, along with hiring minorities and women, would you say that Allan Pinkerton had hired an inexperienced, unpracticed, and amateur young person to chase down two well-experienced and hardened mountain men?"

"I object, Your Honor!" Rawlings said, shooting to his feet.

"And what grounds?" Judge Smith asked.

"Council for the defense was leading the witness!"

"Yes, I agree, but I want to hear her answer," Smith said.

"Well, Mrs. Spells, was your boy inexperienced, an amateur and unpracticed in the job of going to the wilds of the Rocky Mountains, and hunting down two rugged and experienced mountain men who had lived in those environs for years?"

"Yes, and when Robbie left, I begged him not to go. I told him, you don't know what you're getting into or what you're going up against, and I fear for your life," Mrs. Spells said and wiped a tear from her eye.

"I am sorry for upsetting you, dear, but what was Robbie's response to your concerns?"

"He said, *'How hard can it be? It ain't like I'm going to the moon, or anything.'*"

"But it was foreign and dangerous environs into which he rode, wasn't it?"

"Babes in the woods," she said.

"I beg your pardon?"

"Babes in the Woods, it was a story I read to Robbie when he was little, you know the tale, don't you?"

"Sorry, I don't," Gass said.

"Well, these children lose their parents and are put into the care of their aunt and uncle, who sell the children to these two bad men, but the weaker of the two kills his partner, and then he simply leaves the children in the woods. They wander around for God knows how long before they simply died of the elements, then the robins came and—" At this point, Mrs. Spells broke down and began to weep.

"You don't have to continue," Gass said, taking her hand.

"No, no, I must, the robins come and covered their dead bodies with the beautiful autumn leaves, and my Robbie was by himself, all by himself, and he got covered all right, but instead of the beautiful colors of autumn, it was white of death, winter snows!" and she fell into Gass's arms across the witness stand and wept like a child.

"We will take a short recess," Judge Smith said.

———

Immanuel and Uzziah were taken into a room off the court, where there were plenty of windows, and the day had progressed. They could not resist sitting by the windows and watching the birds hopping along the window sills, pecking at whatever was there.

"I wish we had some crumbs," Uzziah said.

Immanuel pulled a small slice of bread from his vest pocket, which he'd saved from breakfast, and the two mountain men broke it up and let it fall from the slightly opened window to the sill. The sparrows were on it in an instant.

"Now, ya got somethin' to eat," Uzziah said, smiling.

Monty Gass walked in, and they turned in his direction.

"This is going better than imagined," he said.

"How can ya gloat, that poor woman!" Uzziah said.

"Yes, I hated that, too," Gass said.

"No, ya didn't," Immanuel interrupted. "It's exactly where ya were leadin' her, yer no better than the men who left the children in the woods. Ya didn't have led her to the place where her son ended up, but ya sure did, and you showed him to her in his death, didn't ya!" Immanuel said.

"Don't you two see, the more we can get this to look exactly like what it was, the more it distances you two from Robert's death."

"Well, we ain't responsible for a man freezing to death ifn he didn't know how to take care of hisself in the winter, in the mountains," Immanuel said.

"But neither of us want ya to ask her anything else, it's sad enough that she had a fool for a son without the whole world knowin'," Uzziah added.

———

They went back in and Monty Gass told Judge Smith that he was through questioning Mrs. Spells.

"We call Kate Warne to the stand, Your Honor," Rawlings said.

Kate was dressed in black. Her dress was long, and the jacket over her cream-colored blouse was accented by a red scarf. Regardless of her drab apparel, she looked radiant.

After being sworn in, she took her seat in the witness box and repeated for the court her name and occupation.

"Did you have as an assignment the finding of the

two men who you thought to be responsible for the death of Robert Spells?"

"Yes, that's right," she said matter-of-factly.

"And did you meet those two men on the paddle wheeler, The Clermont?"

"I did," she answered, and Uzziah thought of his flirting with her when she was about to arrest him and shook his head.

"And how did that come about in your own words?"

"Well, I was sitting in the dark having a glass of whiskey." There was a sort of gasp in the courtroom when she said that. "Women do drink, you know, and fairly soon, we'll vote," she added, and there was a babbling in the courtroom.

"Order! Order in the court!" Judge Smith said and banged his gavel hard on the bench.

"Miss Warne, please limit your responses to those asked of you, if you would?"

"Certainly, Your Honor," she said.

"Then, please continue," Judge Smith advised her.

"As I said, I was sitting where hardly anyone could see me, and I struck up a conversation with this mountain man type."

"And is that person present in this courtroom?" Rawlings asked.

"Of course, he's the heavier one sitting next to the old one," she said and smiled at both of the partners.

They looked at each other, and you could almost hear them saying to themselves, *She called ya fat*, and *she called ya old*.

"Let the record show that Miss Warne has pointed out Uzziah O'Bannon. And where was Immanuel at that time?"

"He was at the table cheating at cards," she said straight-faced.

"That's a damned lie!" Immanuel stood up and shouted.

"Order, order in my court. Mr. Jones, you will be gagged if you speak out without being spoken to in my court. Do you understand?"

"Sorry, out west we shot people at a card table who call us cheaters," Immanuel explained, and Kate Warne smiled big, and so did Allan Pinkerton, sitting in the courtroom.

Monty Gass grabbed Immanuel's arm and pulled him back down to his seat.

"Continue, Miss Warne," Rawlings said. He was glad, obviously, they had planned the insult and knew what outbreak they would get from the mountain men.

"Well, the fat one, he wanted to get me back to my room," she said.

"What do you mean?" Rawlings asked.

"He was interested in putting the devil into hell," she managed to say without smiling.

"How did you know that?"

"A woman knows such things," Warne said, and Immanuel coughed and his loud cough sounded like, *Whore!*

———

After a short break, the trial started again, but this time, Immanuel James Jones was gagged.

"So, what happened when you noticed that Uzziah O'Bannon wanted to get you to put the devil back in hell?" Rawlings asked.

"Well, I got him to talking, and before long, he just told me his name, just like that, even though we had a warrant out for him and his partner. Then, when he reached over to hold my hand to lead me to my room, I pulled my derringer and arrested him. He yelled out some nonsense. 'Flummadiddle!'" she yelled, and half the courtroom started chuckling.

"Order, order in my court!" Smith yelled, banging the gavel on the bench.

"So, after the word, which I will not repeat, was yelled, what happened?" Rawling asked.

"Well, I already had the cuffs on Uzziah, and Immanuel grabbed his paper winnings off the table and ran for the railing on the opposite side of the Hurricane Deck."

"Wasn't your partner Tom Branch there in the saloon?"

"Yes, and as many shots as Tom fired at Immanuel, you'd have thought he would have resembled a sieve, but Immanuel jumped into the Missouri and got away."

"At least that's what you thought at the time, correct?"

"Hey, Judge Smith, could you have the prosecutor be quiet so I can tell the story?"

Both Judge Smith and Rawlings looked at each other.

"I think you heard the young lady," the judge said.

"Yeah, so Tom Branch and a bunch of other men who were anxious for some action shot a lot of lead into the Missouri River, hoping to hit the man who had cheated so much at cards, but I thought Immanuel had swam to the shore and skedaddled. Instead, he swam under the vessel and around to the back of the paddle wheeler, where a man can have the sense knocked out of him, and swimming under the paddle as it was moving, he grabbed it and pulled himself up on the ship.

"Then he broke into the room of an English gentleman, shaved his beard, not the English gentleman's, but his own, to look just like the Englishman. Then he dressed in the man's clothes and return to the saloon, and when he saw what cabin Tom Branch went into, he followed him, broke down the door, and with Agent Branch's guns blasting away at him, Immanuel shot the gun from Tom's hand and grabbed me and threatened me with killing if I didn't release his partner!"

There was general applause in the courtroom as everyone appreciated a good story, and Immanuel stood up, gagged and all, and bowed to the gallery and then, the jury. There were hoots of laughter at Immanuel's antics.

———

There was a short break, and when the court resumed, Immanuel was tied to his chair.

"So, was that the end of your involvement with these two desperados?" Rawlings asked Miss Warne.

"I object, Your Honor, though, certainly my clients were desperate and reckless, they have never been labeled desperados!"

"Overruled, I believe their behavior here today has been enough to say they might indeed be desperados!"

"Really, Your Honor!" Monty Gass stood and objected

"Really, and unless you'd like to defend these two

gagged and tied to a chair, I would hope you would remember court protocol."

"Yes, Your Honor," Monty Gass said and sat back down.

"What was the question?" Kate Warne asked, enjoying what was happening in the courtroom.

"After their escape, was that the last that those two men had to do with the paddle wheeler?" Rawlings asked.

"Oh no, they rode their horses out and shot up the mechanism of the paddle wheeler and rendered The Clermont useless in the water."

"And could some of those shots have endangered the passengers of The Clermont?"

"Most certainly, a 54-caliber slug can render a lot of damage to human flesh."

"Thank you, that's all the questions I have for Miss Warne," Rawlings said and returned to his seat.

Immanuel was jumping up and down in his chair and trying to get Monty Gass's attention.

"Your Honor," Monty said, "I request a short recess."

"Ten minutes," Judge Smith said.

10

They had taken the gag off Immanuel and untied him to get him out of the courtroom. Once the two were taken to the side room and Monty joined them, Immanuel wheeled around at him.

"That bitch is full of Satan, that's what she is! First off, her man Tom Branch don't shoot with his gun, he shoots with his Johnson, and that's the only thing that whore cares about. She weren't drinking whiskey, it were wine, right, Uzziah?"

"He's right, it was wine, but most of what she told was truth as far as I know."

"And from the distance we shot at The Clermont, there was no way she could know without a doubt that we was the one doin' the shootin'!" Immanuel filled in.

"But you were the ones, right?" Gass asked.

Uzziah and Immanuel looked at each other. "Yeah," Immanuel said, "We wrecked that paddle wheeler that's a fer sure!"

"Well, it really doesn't matter about what you did to the paddle wheeler. What we have to establish is the fact that Robert Spells's death was, in essence, an accidental death or possibly self-inflicted."

"Ya mean like suey-side?" Uzziah asked.

"Face it, partner, ya can't fix dumb," Immanuel added.

The door to the room where they'd taken the defendants opened and the bailiff stuck his head in. "There's somebody here to see you," he said.

"Okay, bring them in," Gass said.

When the door opened, Monty Gass knew who the elderly gentleman was, but both Uzziah and Immanuel just looked at him. Gass stood up. "Mr. President," he said with a sort of awe.

"Former President Jackson," Jackson said, then added, "That damned fool Van Buren sits in my chair now. You two must be Immanuel James Jones and Uzziah Ferguson O'Bannon, right?" Jackson said and hung his hickory cane on his left arm as he extended his right to shake hands with them. All three of them pumped like real men were supposed to, and Jackson was smiling the whole time.

"What are you doing here, Mr. President?" Gass asked politely.

"Jefferson's granddaughter helped me get elected, and she wrote me a note about this chere trial. It's a damned shame what's happenin' here, I was in the anteroom listenin' to that soiled dove of a Pinkerton Agent." At that, Immanuel laughed loudly. "Yeah, son, you were right, she'd sell everything she had to get ahead, beware of women like that. Anyways, if I can take the stand, you rest yer case, and I think this whole thing'll be over."

"But I don't think the prosecution is finished presenting the evidence, Mr. President."

"What evidence? The boy was out of his element, and it cost him his life. He might as well shot hisself, I won't say that, but I got somethin' to say about men like these two." He pointed at Uzziah and Immanuel, and then added, "I sure does."

———

When the court reconvened, Monty Gass stood.

"Your Honor, may I approach the bench?"

Judge Smith had seen former President Andrew Jackson in the back of the courtroom when they had come from recess, and if Smith was anything, he was a political creature. He knew if he crossed the former president, his political career might as well be in the toilet.

"Come, come, and you too, Rawlings," Smith said.

The prosecutor looked puzzled and walked to the bench.

"I would like to see you, Your Honor, with a guest in your chambers," Gass asked politely.

"Sure, come on, gentlemen," Judge Smith said.

———

The two lawyers, Rawlings and Gass, walked toward the judge's chambers, and when Judge Smith entered, he was not at all surprised that former President Andrew Jackson was already seated in there, albeit comfortably in the back corner of the big office, trying to be as unobtrusive as possible.

Behind Judge Smith was Rawlings, then Gass. Rawlings walked in and saw the man in the corner, first not recognizing him, then doing so.

"By the gods, sir, I would have recognized you anywhere," Rawlings said, extending his hand.

Jackson extended his hand and shook Rawlings's proffered hand, then it dawned on Rawlings and he turned to Judge Smith.

"This doesn't mean—"

"Let's face it, Mr. Rawlings, there is little probable cause in what witnesses have said to this point," Judge Smith said, then added, "It's just the former president wishes to go on the record at this trial."

"Buy why?" Rawlings asked Jackson, as he turned again toward the man.

"Y'all soon know, sonny," was all Jackson said.

"I assume, Mr. Gass, that this is all right with you and your defendants?"

"Of course, Your Honor."

"I think this is setting a dangerous precedent," Rawlings objected.

"We'll see," was all Judge Smith said as he went to the door and opened it for former President Jackson.

When the four men entered the courtroom, a buzz of conversation erupted, the former president being recognized. Kate Warne and Allan Pinkerton got up out of their seats and were visibly shaken. It was obvious that Jackson having been in the judge's chambers meant something, and they weren't exactly sure what it meant.

It had been said that from that day forward, Allan Pinkerton made it a habit to get as close to the White House as possible, eventually starting the Secret Service and guarding the 16th President during the nation's greatest trials.

Jackson did not sit down as yet, but stood in front of the witness stand, and the bailiff nearly fell over himself going to him, then forgetting his Bible, went back, got it, and Jackson was sworn in. That Bible was never again used by the bailiff, but tucked away as a family heirloom.

Mr. Gass sat at the defense table and asked the former president one question: "Why are you here today, President Andrew Jackson?"

"Thank ye for havin' me, and that thanks goes out to every man jack and ya ladies, too, in this court. I was bern nine years afore this country wrestled its freedom from the British Empire. Any man jack who knows me knows I hates the British and always will, I can only hope that when I get to heaven most of them have been relegated to the nether regions." There was a smattering of chuckles among the gallery, but Judge Smith himself had laughed, so why bother to bang the gavel and interrupt.

"I was livin' in the Carolinas when the British invaded in 1780. Theys put me in prison and"—he laughed to himself here—"theys expected me to shine the boots of the commandin' officer among the British troops. I tells the man what he could do with his boots, and volunteered to put them there, if he'd let me. For that bit of sass, I was slapped across me face with his sword. I's still have the mark to this day," he said as his right hand went up and touched the scar on his left cheek.

"My ma and two brothers, God rest their souls, were killed by the British durin' that invasion, being starved to death and unable to fight off disease. So's as ya can see, I have no cotton with those from England and ne'er will.

"I studied law in what is now known as the Volunteer State, and did quite well gettin' paid for things people ought to have known was wrong. When the War of 1812 broke out and the Brits had the gall to set fur to Washington, I offered my 50,000 troops, all good and loyal men, for the invasion of Canada. The government moved slowly, as it always does, and finally me and my troops were called into a conflict with the Creek Injuns, who were in alliance with the Brits for God knows what reason.

"My command fought the Creek Injuns fer five months and beat their moccasins off at the Battle of Tohopeka. That victory were so decisive that the Creek Injuns never again threatened no American settlers. I became, in some fool's imaginations, *the hero of the west.*

"What I did next nobody coulda guessed. I marched my army south toward Pensacola, which was then full of them Spaniards, but my thinking was clear. Spain had entered into a pact with the Brits, and as fer as I was concerned, we was in a war with 'em, too. When I got to Pensacola, the Brits had run like the no-good sons-a-bitches they are and shipped off to New Orleans, which was then also under the same Spanish bastards.

"The Battle of New Orleans, where we were outnumbered by 2,300 British troops, and we took the day. They ran from us to the sea, where they boarded ships and got the hell outta there. Sixty-two dead patriots were lost to us, but the scourge of the earth, the Brits, had 2,034 dead scattered from where we first engaged them to the sea, and among their dead was their General Edward Pakenham and Major General Gibbs. I was then called more than *the hero of the west*, I was called *the hero of the nation*. Now, back then, the treaty which ended the War of 1812 was signed on the 24th of December, fifteen days before the 8th of January 1815. So, in effect, all those Brits that died died after the War of 1812 was over, but hey, give me a chance to kill a Brit, and I'll sure 'nough take it!

"And this is what brings me to the two men sitting at the table for the defense. It had been in 1803 when President Thomas Jefferson had made the Louisiana Purchase, and then President Jefferson sent out his now famous expedition, and one of the men on that expedition, Patrick Gass, is in the gallery today. If this country had lost the Battle of New Orleans, it has been suggested that the Louisiana Purchase would have been lost to the British, and that would have been a terrible loss."

At this point, Jackson sat down on the table for the prosecution and rested from his pacing back and forth but still used his hickory as one might use a pointer in a lecture.

"I was the first president elected by the common man—that's each and every one of you sittin' out there, and you in the jury. And I am proud to say that I am a common man, ain't nothin' wrong with being common. There's common sense, which seems to be lacking in this case, and the common good, common knowledge, common interest, common folk, and, of course, the common enemy, which is the way I view the British, and common friends, the way I view these men sitting at the other table.

"This country is a miracle wrought by God Almighty Himself. It was not conceived by the powers that now threaten it, the government has grown too big, and the companies that are supposed to be making goods for the citizens of this country are profiting too much. We, the little man, the common people, are not being considered.

"It were common men who resented taxation without representation, and common men who threw British tea into Boston harbor. And it were common men, farmers and the like, who gathered on the common green in Lexington just before dawn on the 29th of July 1775, and it were commoners who fired the shots that were heard around the world. Yes, we had to retreat at first, we were vastly outnumbered, so we went to Concord, where the British thought that our militia was storing supplies for treasonous acts against the crown. And while they searched, our militia regrouped and we drove each one of those mother's sons to Boston, where we blocked the access to the sea and the Siege of Boston began. And at the age of thirteen years, I, another common man, was proud to serve my country in that War of Independence.

"It was men like you and me who drove the largest and most powerful army to their knees, and after a great and mighty struggle led by our first president, George Washington, we won our common independence.

"And when I was elected, we instituted policies which kept the Second National Bank from gaining a foothold because they opposed our manifest destiny, our commonness, they opposed our expansion into the west. Jacksonian democracy opposed the eastern power center of this country and moved it to the western frontier.

"Without my presidency, which, I'll admit, was not a success with everyone, but without it, the little man, the common man, would never have been invited into the White House after my victory in 1829, and the party there was so raucous that I left and slept in a Washington hotel that night. But, Lord, did the common man celebrate that day!

"And men like Immanuel James Jones, who is the son of Patrick Gass and a Mandan woman at Fort Mandan, and Uzziah Ferguson O'Bannon, whose father and mother are farmers in the Shenandoah Valley, men like these two have made it their life's work to go into the territories discovered by Lewis and Clark and make those territories their homes. Without such men, those same territories would have again been lost to the French or British during the fur trading years.

"It had been said that mountain men have no law, that they lived a hedonistic existence, and they are a law unto themselves, but who was it that pulled the assassin Richard Lawrence off me and wrestled him to the ground, none other than a frontiersman, mountain man, if you will, Congressman Davy Crockett. And was it not this same great patriot, frontiersman, and member of the House of Representatives, who died in the Texas Revolution at the Alamo on March 6, 1836, at the age of only forty-nine? That, my friends, was only a scant half dozen years ago.

"Having been informed of this trial of these frontiersmen by the granddaughter of President Jefferson, Martha Jefferson Randolph, I could not sit idly by and have them railroaded neither onto the gallows nor into the bowels of imprisonment.

"Mrs. Samantha Spells, I, as a former president of these United States, so apologize for the death by the elements of nature of your son, Pinkerton Agent Robert Spells. It should never have happened, but you, sir!" At this point, Andrew Jackson swung his hickory cane around and pointed at Allan Pinkerton. "You should never have sent an inexperienced man out into the wilderness. Why, if I had taken inexperienced troops instead of the hardened, experienced men whom I marched into New Orleans with, well, the outcome might have been very different for this nation.

"And finally, if this court is to judge these two men worthy of death and hanging by the neck, then quite frankly, you might as well hang Ole Hickory himself!"

There was thunderous applause as Jackson limped over to the table for the defense, sat in a chair between Uzziah and Immanuel, and put his arms around them.

"Your honor, I still must object to this testimony, it is prejudicial and sways the jury unduly. I wish to call for a mistrial," Rawlings said, knowing that with a mistrial, the defendants could be tried again for this same crime.

"I find that there is no probable cause for a mistrial, nor, in fact, was there probable cause in arresting and detaining these two men, so the verdict in this case is simple. Case dismissed!" Judge Smith said, and his gavel rang out all over the courtroom.

11

The Grand Wolverine Hotel's dining room had one large table reserved under the name Patrick Gass. Once seated, those at the table were Patrick Gass, his son, Monty, Sean O'Bannon, his two sons, Raymond and Hank, Edgar Allan Poe and his wife, Ginny, and of course, Immanuel James Jones and Uzziah Ferguson O'Bannon.

Uzziah and Immanuel had had baths and stayed at the hotel and were now celebrating their victorious day in count.

Both fathers had gladly seen to their son's new clothes, which bespoke men of substance and not men from the mountains of the Rockies. Yet, the long black coats, the matching vests, and shirts with puffy sleeves still said something besides back east. Beneath the coats, they had gun belts, and regardless of where they were, they carried their Hawken rifles with powder horns and shot. Neither had shaved their beards, but they had had their hair pulled back in the fashion of the day, and wore wide-brimmed western cowpuncher hats, which remained on their heads at the table as opposed to all the others who had taken their hats off.

"Why are your hats still on?" It was Uzziah pa who asked that question.

"Well, partner, ya mind ifn I answer this?" Immanuel asked Uzziah.

"Gored ahead," Uzziah joked, and Immanuel chuckled.

"Me and Uzziah have found out over the years, that there's only one time ya take yer chapeau, as the French say, off, and that is when you are about to enter the bed of a lady friend—"

"And sometimes, it don't come off then!" Uzziah interjected, and the group of men shook with raucous laughter.

"But here's the real reason," Uzziah continued. "Ya never know when yer gonna hafta make a quick exit and ya won't have time fer finding yer hat."

Immanuel pointed across the round table at Uzziah. He had seated himself beside the only woman at the table, Virginia Poe, and had been flirting with her since he sat down.

"I really feel as if I need to pay you back, Patrick, for all the expenses. First, the situation in St. Louis resolved itself without my intervention or knowledge, and secondly, at the trial I was simply a bystander, much like those in the gallery," Poe interjected.

"We wouldn't have done it without you, Poe, and we hope you'll keep us in mind as your literary career takes off," Patrick said, and there was rapping on the table.

"What's with the rapping on the table? I remember you all doing it when William Clark was here?"

They all rapped on the table again, and Poe looked like he was seeing something a thousand miles away. "Well, it's nice here with company, but I can imagine being alone in my house, late at night, and hearing such a rapping on my chamber door."

"Yeah, well, ya never know who that could be, do ya?" Immanuel said, raising his glass. "A toast, that whenever someone comes rapping at our door and ya open it, there will be only darkness and nothin' more,"

They all raised their glasses, but Uzziah could tell that Immanuel was toasting Poe's wife, Virginia, whom he refused to call Ginny. Uzziah simply hoped that his partner would not drink enough to want to boondoggle with her.

The celebratory meal went well, and Immanuel managed to keep his hands off Virginia Poe, who was young enough to be his granddaughter. The surprise of the evening was when Patrick Gass stood up and made an announcement.

"May I have your attention? Obviously, I am thrilled not to attend the hanging of my son Immanuel and his partner Uzziah. But I have been thinking, and that's usually followed by some ruminations which go beyond simple relief. I believe my son and his partner have been spared in order for them to do me and our family a great service. Just as President Jefferson sent Lewis and Clark on the Corps of Discovery Expedition, I wish to send these two men on another expedition, this time to the southernmost coast of this country, specifically to New Orleans.

"I started thinking about this when former President Jackson spoke about the Battle for New Orleans, and what it meant to us as a country. The population of

Baltimore, where my son Monty and I live with our families, is the same as New Orleans—102,000 people. I feel that the business opportunities in New Orleans are about to explode, and I would like to invest monies down there. Would you, Immanuel, my son from a Mandan woman, would you and your partner Uzziah consider going down there and scouting out opportunities for both our families?"

Every eye at the table had gone to the two mountain men. This had been sprung on them without any warning. In a way, after spending nearly two months in windowless cells, all they wanted to do was to escape back to their mountains. Both men looked at each other.

Uzziah wasn't really interested. The monies to be invested would come mostly from the Gass family, and he worried about Immanuel. He wasn't getting any younger, and he feared that if his partner got to a place where the Creole women were noted for their beauty, and the rum, which was imported from the Caribbean, was known for its abundance. Uzziah felt that things could go south in another way.

The two partners had started out meeting in St. Louis, where Immanuel had come to sell his beaver pelts, and then they had gone to the mountains. They had been accused of a murder which they did commit, then those charges were essentially no longer expedient for the city of St. Louis to prosecute. Then, Robert Spells's death had been pinned on them, when they had done the best they could for the young man, given him a horse, firearms, supplies, and set him on the eastern slopes, all he had to do was follow the rising sun.

For the first time since their first meeting, they were free men. Free not only in location, but from the law which seemed always to be on their heels. Somehow, to Uzziah, this offer of jobs investing monies from Immanuel's father seemed like a trap. They would take the money, travel to New Orleans, and then the harpies, those mythical creatures which in Shakespeare's play The Tempest, had tortured the antagonists of the play. Uzziah was totally against this idea put forth by Immanuel's father, Patrick Gass, and hoped by the way he was looking at his partner that he understood this.

"That sounds like a fabulous idea, Pa, me and Uzziah in the Paris of the South!" Immanuel said, once again raising his glass in a toast with everyone else at the table. No one noticed that Uzziah's glass was never picked up.

———

Uzziah knew that the first chance Immanuel got to gamble his father's money, he would. But instead of losing on the grand paddle wheelers, and they were so much more luxurious than those sailing on the Mighty Mo, Immanuel became the life of the party. His gambling seemed to be contrary to any rules of chance. It seemed the drunker he got, the easier he won, and Uzziah and he shared a room on board the vessel. One night after a night of drinking, gambling, and carousing, Uzziah could stand it no longer.

"We can't go on like this?" he said from his bunk.

Immanuel had just sent a woman back to her cabin after making love to her while supposedly Uzziah slept.

"Okay, I'll get my own room," Immanuel said.

"I don't mean that."

"What do ya mean?"

"You could have already gambled away all the money your pa gave you to invest!"

"*Could have*, would be the operative words in that string of spit."

"Don't ya see?"

"See what? We ain't ever been so flush, we got money galore, the women, my God did ya see that one Creole bitch, ifn she weren't with that man of hers, I tell you!"

"Don't ya see where this is agoin'?"

"Yeah, straight down to New O where we will make a killin' and have women from all sort of places fallin' into our beds, and the investments we make will further our pa's fortunes—"

"Stop! Just stop," Uzziah said, getting out of his bunk and sitting at the table in the suite of rooms.

"I kinda thought ya'd be like this, yer an old woman, Uzziah, and maybe ya weren't meant fer no highlife? Ever think of that?"

"Yeah, as a matter of fact, I have. Just promise me one thing."

"What, ya old bag?"

"Y'all try to maintain some sense of decorum and do what's right by yer pa."

"Yeah, yeah, my pa, ya mean the man that found comfort in a squaw's arms and other places, then when she was pregnant, left her to go explorin', and after findin' out I'd been taken by the Injuns, just thought, '*Oh well?*' Ya mean that pa?"

"Immanuel, maybe we should just go back to our cabins in the mountains—"

"The ones that were blown to shite by our so-called mountain man friends, those cabins?"

"We can rebuild."

"Why rebuild in the wilderness when the heart of the Paris of the South will welcome us with open arms?"

"This will end badly?"

"Well," Immanuel said, reaching across and pinching Uzziah's cheek, "ifn ya can't take the heat, get the hell outta the kitchen!"

Uzziah batted Immanuel's hard-pinching hand away from his face. "This is the you I don't much like."

"Well, Shadow is down there in his stall, and ya can get off this floatin' party any time ya like. Me, I'm refreshed and think my Johnson could probably do another one, I'm gonna go up into the saloon and gamble my ass off while searching for another ass to split," Immanuel said.

"Yer makin' a mistake, here, partner," Uzziah urged for the last time.

"No, partner, yer in the mistake makin' business. Why, without me with ya in those Rocky Mountains, ya wouldn't stand a snowball's chance in hell. I made ya into a mountain man, yer forgettin' that, ain't ya. Yer forgettin' how many times I pulled yer arse outta the fires which you created. It's me that made ya what ya are today, and without yours truly, ya don't amount to much asides a farmer with no field to plow. Now, get yer arse up and come with me to party the rest of the night away, young son, what do ya say?"

"I ain't yer son, old man," Uzziah said.

Immanuel's face turned crimson as he thought about beating the ever-living tar out of the fat man seated at his table, but instead, he finished dressing and went out, slamming the door behind him.

Uzziah knew there would be another wood stop soon. He got all his belongings together, leaving behind the fancy clothes, which he piled on the table, and topped them off with the new shiny pair of boots. He put his long johns back on and got dressed in his deerskins. When he put them on, his hands went over them and he smiled. He felt like he was back in his own skin again. He packed his saddlebags with as much as he thought he needed, made sure his Hawken was loaded and he had plenty of powder and shot, and walked down to the stables on the main deck. He could hear Immanuel's raucous voice swearing about something, and everybody laughing with him, at him?

The Black man, who was in his forties, saw Uzziah coming toward his stables.

"What's up, massa, ya gettin' off?"

"Yes, I am."

"Wood station just up ahead, which hass is yourn?"

"The black stallion, Shadow."

"That is a beautiful hoss, but he don't like many."

"No, he's all mine and I'm all hisn," Uzziah said, thinking that he was talking to the first sensible person he'd talked to in a good while.

"I'll be glad to saddle the beast," the Black man said, smiling.

"Here's fer yer trouble," Uzziah said and handed him a silver dollar.

"No, that's too much," the Black man protested.

"It's just right. Say, what's yer name?" Uzziah asked.

"Moses, but most just call me Mose."

Moses went back, saddled Shadow, and walked out with the bit in his hand. As Uzziah put the bit in his horse's mouth and mounted up, he looked down at Moses, who was putting the gang plank down so he could throw wood up on the deck from the wood station.

Just as Uzziah was about to have Shadow step on the gangplank, he looked down at Moses. "Say, thanks for bringing the People of God out of captivity and into the land of milk and honey."

Moses didn't seem to understand at first, then, remembering scripture, smiled and said, "You's welcome, glad I done it."

"Me, too, my friend, me, too," Uzziah said as he clicked up Shadow and the horse stepped up on the gangplank.

Uzziah rode off the ship and onto solid ground, and found the road that led north toward St. Louis, where they'd come from. First, he'd ride to Columbus, Ohio, and tell Benjamin's ma, Loretta Stevens, that her eldest had died like a man. Died like a man in Uzziah's arms, that's what he would tell her. After all, hadn't he promised that to Benjamin right before they hung him? Uzziah could hear the chucking of the wood which Moses was throwing up on the ship, and it reminded him of when he and Immanuel had done the same to gain passage once. He guessed those days were over, still, smiling to himself, *good memories all around*, he thought.

———

Upstairs in the saloon, and sitting at the card table, Immanuel was winning again, and he had that Creole woman hanging on him. His drink was full, just as full as that dark quim was going to be when he took her, he was sure of that.

Someone said something funny, and Immanuel laughed hard. Then the fancy cigar he had clamped between his teeth fell from his mouth as his left arm numbed and he grabbed at his chest. The Creole woman screamed, and there just happened to be a doctor at the same table, losing badly to Immanuel. He had taken quite a hit from this rough man, but he had also taken an oath. *"First, do no harm,"* it started out.

He had Immanuel down on the floor, and the tie around his neck loosened, and his vest pulled back.

"What's wrong?" the Creole woman asked with that strange accent. She, too, had dreamed of having a big White man like that.

"Angina pectoris," the doctor had said, and she thought he must be a foreigner, but he was just giving the proper name of what would later be called a heart attack.

"Will he live?" she asked the foreign doctor.

"If he can stay alive till we get him to New Orleans," he said, administering to Immanuel.

"Get my partner, Uzziah, he's in this suite." Immanuel handed a key to the Creole woman, and she ran down to the numbered suite which matched the number on the key.

"Just relax, son, if God is with ya, y'all live," the doctor said, and Immanuel sure hoped Uzziah would get there soon, he had a mighty big plate of crow to eat, and he didn't much cotton to eating alone.

A LOOK AT BOOK SIX: UZZIAH MEETS THE PROPHET
A UZZIAH MOUNTAIN MAN WESTERN DOUBLE

Time drove them apart. Trouble always brings them back together.

After parting ways on a Mississippi paddle wheeler, Uzziah O'Bannon and Immanuel Jones ride separate trails, both unsure if their paths will ever cross again. Uzziah, restless and disillusioned, leaves the boat and heads north, eventually drawn into the Mormon settlement of Nauvoo. There, he finds unexpected purpose, and a reason to stay—until tragedy strikes, and he must choose between safety and conviction.

Immanuel, still aboard, falls gravely ill. Taken to Charity Hospital in New Orleans, he recovers slowly with help from Dr. Gateaux and the doctor's granddaughter. But city life wears thin. When his estranged father Patrick Gass arrives, Immanuel knows it's time to ride again. After settling his affairs, he heads west, unsure of Uzziah's fate or direction.

Their trails wind through loss and violence. Uzziah serves briefly as deputy sheriff in Jefferson City before heading back to the Rockies with an elderly Mohawk—unsure if Immanuel made it home, or if the high country is now just a memory.

Will years of separation forge stronger bonds, or leave nothing worth returning to?

This two-book bundle includes the eleventh and twelfth novels in the Uzziah Mountain Man *series.*

AVAILABLE JANUARY 2026

ABOUT THE AUTHORS

He was good looking and could sell ice to eskimos. But ... writing asked something else from him. He would have to corral his interest in being free. Writing would take him to a place where he was tamed, but also able to actually tell a story.

After the first two weeks at the Yale School of Drama, he called the head of the playwriting department, Milan Stitt and told him he was quitting. Milan invited him to lunch at a nearby Mexican restaurant in New Haven. He told the man who had had plays on Broadway that he wanted to be a free writer. Milan smiled, then explained the way to freedom was always through discipline.

Something in him clicked and it all began to make sense.

Three years later, when he received his MFA in playwriting, he received the much coveted Cole Porter Prize for Excellence in Writing.

Enter a woman, years later, when the first 'J' in J.J. Bonham, Jack Bonham, had written thirty screenplays in 7 years and had one optioned which looked like it actually might be done.

Unlike Milan Stitt, this woman had no plays on Broadway, but was a divorced mother of four grown children. She loved soaps, and was an ardent watcher of the same. In the years of her devotion to watching she developed an uncanny ability to discern plot and analyze character. Uncanny, really better than any of his teachers at Yale.

They, Jack & Judy, the other 'J' in J.J. Bonham, married in Buffalo Springs, Colorado. While teaching elementary school in Denver they read the same novella and looking up and into each other's eyes, realizing something. They could do that.

Thirteen years later they had written nearly 200 novels. Westerns mostly because that was who they were – a misplaced couple from the 19th Century who saw life in a western justice sort of way. They danced in Virgina City, Montana. Dances from a different time and place, but still their time and place.

Now, they live in the Bitterroot Valley on five acres and looking out the office window as he puts this together for them, he can see the thunderstorm marching across the Sapphire Mountains. Earlier, sitting on the porch, she had said something about the crack of lightning years before as they said vows of love in Buffalo Springs. He remembered.